RSVIP SERVICES, LLC

This book is a work of fiction. Names, characters, places and incidents are either products of the author's imagination or are used fictitiously. Any resemblance to actual events or locales or persons, living or dead is entirely coincidental.

Copyright © 2012 by Tanisha Janice Beecher

Synopsis

The lives of several men have been turned upside down by one woman. Lexi.

Approximately eight years ago when beautiful Lexi Jones arrived in America, a series of unfavorable events aroused her dark side. After quickly realizing that she'd been deceived, and that the glorious American lifestyle she'd been promised while living in Jamaica, would never materialize, she set out on a path for revenge against one man, Everhard. Her stepfather.

In her quest for revenge, and mission to survive in America, Lexi devastated many, but in the end, revenge was served. Her nightmare was believed to have ended and she was satisfied.

Flash-forward to the present, eight years later, as Lexi discovers her life was now in danger. Someone was after her and her family. One threatening phone call is all it would take to set the stage for her new nightmare. Whoever was after her was out for blood. This time around, someone sought vengeance against Lexi. Will she survive this time around, when the only verdict is vengeance?

Vengeance Is the Only Verdict:

It's **L E X I** Again

2nd Edition

Tanisha Beecher

Praises for "The Chronicles of Lexi: What a Girl Would Do to Survive in America"

- Rated 5 Out of 5 Stars By OOSABookClub

    Revenge Best Served...Deadly

    "Tanisha Beecher's "The Chronicles of Lexi: What a Girl Would Do to Survive in America" is a must read. It will catch readers' attention from very early on. It's a story of people who are envious, jealous and greedy and will stop at nothing to get what they want. The plot, twists and turns in this book will have you overwhelmed with the amount of treachery and leaves you wanting more. If you love reading about drama, setups, love and lies, then take a seat and enjoy the ride from the wild side."

    Reviewed by: KaTina-

- "...Girl the book is good... to be honest I can't wait for your next book. Put me on the list and notify me as soon as it is off the press lol."

    Dahlia~

A WORD FROM THE AUTHOR

Dear readers:

First, let me begin by welcoming you to these pages, and to my work. Before you continue, there are a few things I'd like to highlight.

This novel is a sequel to "The Chronicles of Lexi: What a Girl Would Do to Survive in America"; however, it was masterfully written to ensure you are not lost if you haven't read part one.

Secondly, for those of you Lexi fans, after the prelude, she does not appear again until chapter nine; however, the first eight chapters will shock you!

Thirdly, this novel hopefully finalizes the 'Lexi Saga'; however, not to worry. My novella, "Sex Anthology", an erotica, is scheduled to be released in December, 2013. "Light Skin, Pretty Hair & Brown Eyes" is scheduled to be released in spring of 2014, and of course, many more to come. Please stay tuned.

Last, but certainly not least, I hope you will enjoy reading the following pages as much as I enjoyed writing them. Please visit my website for more information: www.tanishabeecher.com.

You know I keep it movin' just for you!
Ya Girl,
Tanisha

PRELUDE
LEXI

Approximately eight years ago, my husband and I endured a most horrific experience—but such is life, right? It was by far, the toughest time we had ever endured. After overcoming such an ordeal, I hoped and prayed with all my heart, and then some, that our past wouldn't come back to haunt us, but it did. By the time you get through these pages, you will have realized just how much damage one's past is capable of producing.

Let me explain how it all went down.

About five years ago, I agreed to testify in court against my ex-boyfriend, Vaughnn. In return, the FBI drummed up an immunity deal so that my testimony could not be used against me. In order to guard my testimony and my life, the federal agency submitted a protection request on my behalf.

A Witness Security Program Application was then presented to the Office of Enforcement Operations, summarizing my testimony against Vaughnn; the threat my testimony could possibly pose to me and my family; and our potential danger to a new community, provided we were relocated.

We later attended a preliminary interview with the United States Marshals Service, where we learnt what our new lives would be like in the Witness Protection Program.

The interview had gone well, and the US Marshals Service submitted its recommendation to the US Attorney General for our protection. After that, we were successfully enlisted into the Witness Protection Program.

My husband, JT; my son, Lexington; and I were protected from any retaliation from Vaughnn, throughout the trial, and beyond; we now had the US Marshals backing us.

My family and I were kept in a holding house for about one year until the trial, when my testimony sealed the deal in Vaughnn's incarceration.

The drama, however, didn't just end there. My husband began to act up, especially after our son was born. See - I was pregnant and had given birth a couple of weeks after Vaughnn's arraignment.

Anyway--like I was saying, immediately after our son was born, my husband had become withdrawn. I know that he loves our son, but JT's sudden peculiar behavior was unrepresentative of the man I'd known nearly all my life, and had been best friends with. I just couldn't, for the life of me, figure out why my husband had suddenly begun to act so crazy.

We moved from Pembroke Pines to Cincinnati, and assumed new identities, which was typical of being in the witness protection program. We were, however, allowed to keep our first names, so we did. Even though I had legally lost my family name, in my heart I would always be Lexi Jones-Miller, wife of JT Miller.

I was glad I didn't have to change my first name or that of my son's. Our first names embodied so much, and too many people had already fallen in love with the name Lexi. So I kept it. My son, Lexington, was named after me—I'm sure you get my drift.

JT kept his name as well; in fact, it wasn't the only thing he'd kept. He had also kept running his mouth about who we were. He continued revealing our identity to the public. The rules of the Witness Protection Program forbade us to make known our true identities to anyone, as it would compromise our safety.

Upon their discovery of JT breaking the rules of the program, the US Marshals relocated us from Tennessee to Cincinnati, and gave us new identities all over again. The only explanation I received was that my husband had been keeping in touch with friends back home in Pembroke Pines, Florida, and had also disclosed our true identities to our new neighbors.

We were updated on the rules and the importance of sticking to them; we were also warned of the consequences of doing otherwise.

One year later, which was three years ago—I hope you understand me so far, we got kicked out of the Witness Protection Program; the reason? JT's violation of the rules— again.

JT then insisted that we return to Pembroke Pines, FL, to live. He assured me that our family would be safe and that enough time had passed for our enemies to forget about us. JT maintained that we had disappeared long enough, and that no one— neither Vaughnn nor his prison posse, would even as much as consider that we dared return.

JT had somehow convinced himself that all attempts against our lives would by now be aborted.

I told myself that our relationship would improve and that JT would stop acting up if I gave in to his demands. So, for the survival of my family, I cooperated with my husband. I had only one condition, that we relocate to Weston instead, which was close enough to Pembroke Pines, FL. He was pleased with that, so we moved back to South Florida.

With the FBI and US Marshals no longer protecting us, the saga begins.

CHAPTER ONE
VAUGHNN

I closed my diary, sat up in bed, and glanced around the stark prison cell in which I'd spent approximately four years already. Four years ago, when the courts had sentenced me to life in prison without any chance of parole, I'd already spent over a year of my life in jail, waiting to be tried and finally sentenced, totaling just over five years since I had lost my freedom.

I observed the toilet that sat barely two feet away from my bed; wondered how I'd really managed to cope for this long in such harsh confines. I also wondered if I could continue to cope with the thought of spending the rest of my life in this place. I'd be here until the day I died--provided I didn't take my own life first.

This was no life, no life for me at all. Right now, I just existed. There was absolutely no reason to live—well, maybe one. Lexi. She was the cause of my ill fate.

For the past five years I'd been dreaming of ways in which to make her suffer. I now had plenty of ideas, as I've had plenty of time to think. Revenge against Lexi had been the only thought that's kept me going all this while; the only thought that's kept me fueled.

I've made attempts in the past to have her assassinated. Once while I was locked up in jail, and twice after I was imprisoned. But she seemed to have fallen off the face of the planet. Seemed as if the FBI was hiding her, but I never gave up hope. I continued to dream of vengeance.

For every prison riot I've been thrown into-- whether voluntarily or involuntarily; for every blow, stab, or poke I've rendered, or has been rendered back to me; for every type of punishment I've inflicted on other cons or has been inflicted on me, all in the name of survival, I blame Lexi. Now, finally, she'd resurfaced. I got word that she was now living in Weston with her punk ass husband and retarded kid.

The idiot husband had opened up a Jamaican restaurant off Flamingo Road and ran a lumber store off SR-84.

I shook my head and furrowed my brows in scorn as my mind wandered back to one week ago, when Olivere Lisken was stabbed several times in his throat with a razor. It all happened so fast. The entire prison was placed on lockdown until the following morning, when members of the Nu Order Gang pinned the murder on Conrad, the Jamaican dude who'd refused to join a group.

Conrad would possibly be facing death row sentencing, and nobody was there to help him. But such was the prison life. There were a set of rules that everyone understood. You either played by the rules, or get seriously hurt or even killed. None of the inmates dared to snitch on fellow inmates, for fear of losing their lives. It was all a dangerous game and I often wondered how much longer I'd survive playing such a game.

I was a member of the Nu Order Gang; had even managed to build a very good rapport with the leader, Atnulu, who had taken a special liking to me. I was always aware of Atnulu's plots against Olivere and Conrad. Matter-of-fact, I was the cause of Olivere's demise. I had stabbed him to death with that razor.

I knew my deeds have been inhumane, even more so since my prison sentence. Whatever values or morals I had remaining had totally dissipated once I landed behind bars. I've had to perform the most malevolent tasks in order to save my ass. My sense of self was now almost dried up, except for the part of me that clung to the hope of taking down Lexi, and all the people she loved.

As a result, I embraced being at the top of this prison's hierarchy, working with Atnulu and other deadly inmates to run the joint. It didn't matter to me that I no longer had a soul—I felt I'd sold it by identifying with the Nu Order clique.

Olivere's murder and Conrad's grave misfortune had been my advance payment to Atnulu, for working with me in the future on the Lexi project. Like I said, the rules could not be broken. Any inmate who incurred a debt, was required to repay, usually promptly, or even in advance, even if it meant working it off on his knees.

Atnulu had all the right contacts within and outside of prison. I hadn't come this far to punk out now.

In the outside world, I was a man of my own rules. I ran my own show; freedom was sweet. But all of that was now water under the bridge because of Lexi.

Lexi Jones was to be blamed for Olivere's murder and Conrad's risk of facing death row.

The sudden sound of footsteps and keys clinking together interrupted me from my thoughts.

"Gibbs!" one of two prison officers shouted, "You have a visitor!"

I jumped to my feet in utter disbelief. I finally had my first visitor after five years of being locked up. No shit! I watched as the guards commenced unlocking the bars.

"Up against the wall; hands behind your back!" the second officer shouted.

Moments later I was shackled and led to an area where I sat in front of what seemed to me like some sort of glazed glass, separating me from my visitor.

I stared blankly at him. He was an average built, high yellow dude, in a three piece suit and tie. He picked up the phone on his end and I picked up mine and listened to what he had to say. By now, my initial feelings of excitement had been replaced by numbness.

"Mr. Gibbs, I'm Humphrey Sharp, your new lawyer."

I glanced at the officers then back at my visitor.

"Go on," I said, eyeing him suspiciously.

"Carlton Fluorentine; have you mailed him your letter yet?"

"Letter? What letter? What are you talkin' about?"

"There are certain court decisions that have been in place for many years now. The Guajardo v. Estelle decision permits inmates to correspond with other inmates throughout the agency"

"I don't have any problems in that area," I replied through gritted teeth. He was beginning to piss me off by the second. Who the hell was this flaming lookin' punk? Why was he here?"

"Calm down Mr. Gibbs, I'm just making sure you're aware of your rights. Wanted you to know you may also utilize the US mail system. I know you are now cut off from the outside world and there are loved ones you'd probably like to stay informed about. Do you understand?"

I didn't understand a thing. I was confused. He was speaking in parables and I still didn't know who he was.

"Let them know that the debt has been satisfied. A new day can be experienced. People shouldn't live in the past when the debt of the past has been settled," he said staring me dead in the eyes.

Say what?

"That's it for now Mr. Gibbs. A very good friend of yours has requested that I review the details surrounding your case—see if there's anything that might have been missed. If you don't hear from me again, it simply means there's no need."

"Guards!" I yelled angrily. The officers responded immediately and escorted me back to my cell. I'd left my visitor sitting there looking like the goon that he was.

CHAPTER TWO
VAUGHNN

"What did Sharp say to you?" Atnulu asked as he joined me and the rest of the gang at the table for dinner.

"What?"

"Sharp. What did he tell you?"

"Wh- how did—"

"Neva mind that; I'll explain later. Just tell me what he said; verbatim."

I did as I was told and started talking. Asking too many questions could make me look weak, and weakness was a definite no-no in this prison facility. As close as Atnulu and I were, I knew he would turn against me in a heartbeat at the slightest sign of weakness.

"He said somethin' 'bout a debt being settled- um—"

"Aight, good," Atnulu said, cutting me off. "The debt is settled then. So, did he say anything about mail correspondence?"

"Matter of fact, yeah. He said that I have the right to utilize the US mail system."

"That's all I needed to know," Atnulu smiled wickedly, as he sucked on his chicken bone.

I took a bite of my meal and chewed in silence. Everybody at the table ate in silence, eyeing each other intermittently.

Every inmate knew that it was best to stay quiet rather than say the wrong shit and get killed.

I could feel Atnulu eyeing me sideways while he ate. I kept my eyes on my food. This was no fucking life.

"Yo, Baldy," he said, turning towards me. "you did a good job back there last week," he lowered his voice to almost a whisper.

"Yeah," I slightly turned towards him, but not too much. My focus remained on my plate.

"The lawyer you spoke to, Sharpe, is a friend of mine," he explained.

"Aigh't," I said nodding my head in approval. See, I'd come to observe that Atnulu was full of himself and full of shit. He lived for praise and people's approval. Of course I kept my opinion to myself.

I knew he wanted to surprise me with the news of having such influential contacts in the outside world. I continued to nod my head while facially expressing awe, so Atnulu continued.

"So, Gibbs, it's like this. Sharpe did a case some time ago representing Rosa Hicks and her husband,

Raymond Hicks, the son of Alfred Hicks, Real Estate Mogul of Miami. It was alleged that Olivere Lisken, the con that you stabbed to death, raped, shot and stabbed Rosa Hicks in front of her husband, before stabbing and shooting him to death.

Their six year old daughter, who was hiding in a closet on the second floor, was also allegedly shot and stabbed to death by Olivere. It was also alleged that Conrad Davis, the con we set up for death row, was a friend of the now deceased Olivere. Conrad had conspired with him to commit the murders. But that's not all. Both men were also involved in trafficking drugs.

Attorney Sharpe represented the Hicks family in court. Being the greedy and arrogant pig that he was, he accepted a pretty sum from the Hicks family and in return assured them that he would see to it that both men received the death penalty. But it didn't go down like that, and the courts sentenced both men to life in prison without chance of parole. Sharpe's ass was now on the line. The Hicks were not pleased with the outcome of the case, and threatened Sharpe."

"Ain't that some shit." I replied. I appeared nonchalant, but my insides were churning. My heart pounded with intensity as I mentally attempted to connect the dots. Atnulu continued.

"I owed Attorney Sharpe a debt. Back in the day, he had found a glitch in one of my appeals while I was on death row. I'd spent five years on death row waiting to hear my execution date. Let me tell you, life on death row was no chicken shit. Anyway, Attorney Sharp stepped in, and in a nut shell, had my sentencing reduced to life in prison without parole. Hence, my debt to him."

"I hear that." I replied easily.

"Mos' def," Atnulu continued, "So when you approached me a few months ago about the Lexi idea, I figured out the perfect way to help you, Sharpe and myself. I made Sharpe an offer. Bottom line: Olivere was my payment to Sharpe. Conrad was the bonus that had turned the tables, leaving Sharpe indebted to me. Now that my debt was settled, he would settle his debt to me, by hooking you up."

"No shit!"

"Yeah, Vaughnn Gibbs, Sharpe was giving you the go-ahead to mail your order for the death of Lexi."

"No shit!"

"Yeah. He was sending me a message through you. That's just the way we operated. The message was to let me know that the Hicks family was finally appeased, now that they felt that justice had been served. And guess what?"

"What?"

"It's all because of you, dawg!" Atnulu grinned.

I grinned too. Hell. This was good news. Though Olivere's death and Conrad's demise weighed heavily on my mind, the thought of such a splendid pay off thrilled me.

Finally, my revenge against Lexi would soon be underway. In a day or two I'd be mailing off my order.

CHAPTER THREE
D-MONEY

Eight Years Ago

My three homeboys and I were paid to do a job. Our boss lady—rich, bourgeois chick—always paid us good money to carry out illegal activities on her behalf. Even though we had been working for her for a while, she never disclosed her name to us. So, we nicknamed her Anonymous and she was cool with that.

Our project was to trail a certain white Escalade. We were to track the driver's movements and intercept any attempts he made at fraternizing with other women; whatever that meant. Based on our instructions, we figured that Anonymous must be the bitter, psycho girlfriend who was willing to do anything to keep tabs on her man.

The driver of the Escalade, whom we presumed to be boss lady's boyfriend, was clean-cut and muscular. He'd been making rounds all night with three dreads in the back of his vehicle. All four of them appeared to be having fun—they seemed to be close friends, or relatives, or somethin'.

So far, my homeboys and I had been carrying out our tasks successfully; matter-of-fact, as a result of our night's success, we had one female tied up in the trunk of the car.

Everything had been going smoothly until the Escalade made a u-turn. We pulled over into a nearby strip mall so we could maintain good vantage, while remaining low-keyed. Fortunate for us, the strip mall was deserted.

We watched as the Escalade got into the immediate turning lane, and made a second u-turn at the traffic light. It continued in the direction prior to making both u-turns, only this time, it slowed to a stop at the bus stop.

Moments later, an unidentified young woman who was sitting at the bus stop, suddenly stood. From our vantage point, we could instantly tell that she was extremely attractive. Her curvaceous silhouette beckoned to us and we were mesmerized.

We continued to watch as the driver of the Escalade exited the vehicle and joined the sexy-looking female at the bus stop.

"There's a female over there?" my homeboy seemed stunned.

"Yeah; what the hell could such a fine ass female be doin' at a bus stop this late at night?" a second homeboy asked.

I checked the time. It was a little after midnight.

"Do buses even run this late at night?" my third homie looked over at me.

I didn't respond. I fired up a blunt and allowed my mind to wander. I thought about the female that was tied up in the trunk of my car. The woman at the bus stop seemed way sexier by far.

I considered my past, the trials of the streets and my ongoing battle with the police. I hate the police. I despised the American system: a system designed to keep a thug like me from moving up in life; a system where the rich got richer, often by using the poor and destitute. Poor people are puppets for the rich.

I, D-Money Jenkins, grew up motherless, fatherless. I guess you could say that I've basically been my own parents. My old lady abandoned me when I was eight years old; and my father? As far as I was concerned, I have no earthly father. The only family I've known since my mother's disappearance is Mama Dukes, who is e'rybody's mama. She's always done what she could for me, but her efforts to rescue others have often stretched her thin. But no matter the cost, Mama Dukes was always there for me, even when I got myself into very sticky situations with the law.

She never failed to bail me out of my predicaments and has never given up on me. She hoped that I would eventually give in to her lectures, go with her to church and turn my life around. Haha, even become a pastor one day. Well, she could continue to hope.

These streets teach lessons. The streets are tough and in order to maneuver the risks and hardships, one has to become rugged. Thugged out. One has to let go of the fear of getting caught breaking the law. One has to become unfazed about hurting others and betraying those closest to you.

In these streets, it's every man for his self. Consequences do not exist. Considering consequences could get in the way of one's survival and everyone wants to survive; so no one considers consequences.

If the means to survival is illicit, then thoughts of consequences only become hindrances to survival-as far as I'm concerned.

I'm all for these streets because they have taught me how to fight the American system my way and win. The system-the American system—doesn't provide for people like me; people who grew up with no mother nor father to support us, teach us right from wrong, guide us, and then send us off to some fancy college once we graduate high school so that we may become progressive, successful, law abidin' citizens who are mostly full of shit.

No, Sir! The system only allows for people who are already rich, or middle class, or were born into rich or middle class families.

As far as I'm concerned, law abidin' poor people are in the same category as unlawful poor people-- well at least where the system is concerned. We are all screwed--one way or another. The poor will continue to be poor, unless we participate in illicit activities, which may propel us out of our destitution.

When the consequences of getting caught are considered, poor people who are suffering continue to suffer. But when we throw consequence through the window, we rise up out of our misery. Should we get caught surviving illicitly, which is the only way per the system, we are robbed of any remaining dignity, thrown into prison where we learn harshly that we shouldn't have used the only survival means available to us.

After punishment has been fully rendered—as if that wasn't payment enough—we are thrown back into a society that completely turns its back on us for having gone to prison in the first place! As if going to prison was our decision. I mean, that is completely backward and unfair. Since there is usually no other way to survive in such a cruel and unforgiving society, we return to so-called unlawfulness. The system is deeply flawed as far as I'm concerned. And dat right there is real tawk.

Mama Dukes seems to think that I'm crazy. She gets scared e'rytime I try to reason with her. She always tries to lecture me into changing my views.

"It's not the system that's flawed; it's the choices we make," she often said. "Many of the prominent men and women of society today were born into poor families, but they are where they are today because they made the choice."

"What choice, Mama Dukes?" I remember asking her in return. "The system don't provide choices for people like us-"

"Yes it do," she'd replied, cutting me off, "the system provides government programs for poor students; financial aid, such as Pell grants for attendance at technical schools, community colleges and universities; as well as church based programs. These are solid options which are available to everyone—the rich, middle class, and poor people like you and me—boy. God gave brains to the poor and he gave brains to the rich. Don't think I'm afraid to slap the taste outta yo' mouth for talking devilish."

Then I'd find a way to make her think I agree, just so she could shut up.

Hmm. Once I heard a bourgeois ass college girl cuss one of my homeboys out. He was trynna holla at her, but she told him, *"I'm not in the least bit intoxicated by your verbosity."*

"Bitch! What the fuck did you just say to me?"

Haha! My homeboy wooped her butt, because none of us knew what she meant.

"The chick is still there, man, he didn't pick her up!" my homeboy shouted, interrupting me from my thoughts.

"How you gon' holla at a chick who's obviously stranded at a bus stop in the wee hours of the morning and just leave her there?" he reasoned.

"Maybe we should go over there and see what's going on," I suggested easily.

"Damn right!" my three homeboys chorused.

I took one last draw from my blunt, discarded its remnant, fired up the engine of my purple, pimped out Cadillac, and headed towards the bus stop. We were about to have some fun with Ms. Sexy. Furthermore, we were only doing what we were being paid to do.

I slowed down as I approached the bus stop to get a good look at her.

She was even sexier than I thought. There she was, just sitting there looking at us all crazy 'n shit.

"Dang she fine!" My boys were enthusiastic.

"Why is she lookin' at us so evil with her fine ass?" one of them asked, grinning.

"Man, ya'll need to just shut up," I said, "Ya'll know that bitch can't see us; our window tint is too dark."

"Well," one of them chimed in sinisterly, "I think she knows that something's about to go down!"

"I'mma turn this bad boy around."

I swerved over into the turning lane as I mimicked the u-turns made earlier by the driver of the Escalade.

My boys were now alive with excitement and were eager for us to finally get to the bus stop. As for me, my johnson was now harder than steel and all I could think about was the lush titties I'd just witnessed rebelling against the silly t-shirt that concealed them.

By the time we made it back to the bus stop, the chick, or should I say, Ms. Sexy, was already up on her feet with the stance of a ninja.

For a while, we just remained in the car. My boys were laughing their tails off. But I wasn't in the mood for laughing. I was in the mood for Ms. Lady over there, so I flew my door open and rushed towards the bus stop beauty; my homeboys followed suit. There was no one around to see us or stop us. It was about to go down.

We could tell she was trying to hide her fear of all four of us; her bravery was enticing. Her body was on point; I couldn't wait to dive into her.

We stole touches as we nudged her towards the back of the bus stop. We were smack talkin' her; she was threatening us. We were laughin' 'n getting all excited.

"Back the fuck up!" she yelled.

"Naw, you back the fuck up," I replied. My homeboys grinned.

I pulled her closer to me and began to rip her clothes from her body.

"Now let me see you back it up fo' big daddy right—"

It all happened so fast. All of a sudden, time stopped so I could process what had just happened to me. I saw light gashing before me as pain seared through my body.

My insides were on fire and the sudden pain was unimaginable. I had just been stabbed.

In shock, I opened my mouth to speak, but no words emerged; only more shock and pain. I was about to die for sure. I looked down at the handle of the knife that protruded from my stomach. I glanced down at my pants that were already beginning to soak from the blood flow that circumvented the knife.

I looked up at the woman who had inflicted such brutality and wondered in mere astonishment if all this shit was real.

I raised my arm to react, but I was too weak; too riddled with pain. Instead, my feet began to give way to the trauma. I attempted to return to my Cadillac, but never made it to my third step. I fell to the ground and my homeboys scattered.

I slowly drifted out of consciousness. In the distance, I could hear voices. They were all shouting.

"She stabbed him?"

"The bitch stabbed him!"

"Let's pounce on this bitch!"

I heard the sound of a vehicle quickly approaching and then gunshots.

"Lexi, did any of these hoodlums hurt you?" someone asked. No response.

"She's in shock. Stewart, help Lexi into the car."

Moments later, the knife was being pulled from my chest. Then there was absolute darkness.

**CHAPTER FOUR
D-MONEY
THE COVER-UP**

Three Days Later

Approximately three days later, I was transferred out of the Intensive Care Unit of Florida Best Care Hospital, where a group of doctors performed surgery to stop the internal bleeding, after which they removed punctured colon from my intestines. They then linked the uninjured segments of my bowels back together—an overall successful operation. Though I was no longer in the ICU, my condition remained critical.

It was then that Mama Dukes visited my bedside with two detectives sandwiching her.
My heart skipped a beat. I was on my death bed; still that hadn't been enough to deter the popos from hounding me.

"How are you feelin', son?" Mama Dukes asked.

"Like I'm dead."

"Don't talk that foolishness, boy."

"Mr. Jenkins, my name is Officer Barkly and this is Officer Lloyd. We are both here to investigate the details surrounding your case. The doctors advised that it was ok to ask you a few questions, alright?"

"I, I guess," I muttered weakly. I was extremely groggy and felt like I was high. It's almost as if I'd just got done smoking some of that good stuff, only better. I didn't realize that hospitals carried such good stuff.

"Mr. Jenkins, did you see the face of the person who stabbed you?" Officer Barkly continued.

"Naw."

"Did you at least get a glimpse?"

"Naw."

"Whynot?"

"Why not what?"

"Why did you not see your assailant's face?"

"It was dark."

"Oh, I see. Was that the only reason?"

"Naw, she was wearing a mask, and—"

"She?" Mr. Officer "Punk" Barkly asked, cutting me off, ready to give me the third degree.

"Yes, it was a she," I confirmed weakly.

"How did you know it was a woman who attacked you? Speaking of attack, what was the cause of the attack?"

"Officers, don't you believe it's too soon to be questioning my son so vigorously?" Mama Dukes asked. "Can't all of this wait until he's recovered in a few days, or at least a few more hours?"

"Well, we can come back tomorrow, but he will have to answer my last question before we go," Officer Lloyd chimed in.

"Repeat the question!" I ordered, growing weaker and sleepier by the millisecond.

"How do you know it was a woman who attacked you, and what do you believe is the reason for the attack?" Barkly barked.

"I dunno the reason why that bitch attacked me."

"Damon Jenkins!"

"Call me D-Money, Mama, I hate the name 'Damon'."

"Mr. Jenkins—"

"Aight officer," I said, cutting off Mr. Barkly, the punk. "Like I said, I dunno why she attacked me. I know my assailant was female because of her appearance."

"What about her appearance?"

"It seemed feminine. Shit—"

"Mr. Jenkins—"

"What, officer? I mean, what else do you want me to say? Even though I'm weak as hell, I'm telling you everything I know. Isn't that enough?"

"Well, did she say anything to you?"

Shit! Think fast D-Money, think fast.

"She didn't say one word to me," I lied.

"So, let me get this straight," Barkly woofed, "a masked assailant who appears to be female, judging by her feminine appearance, for no apparent reason attacks, stabs and leaves you for dead at a bus stop. Correct?"

"Correct," I muttered.

"Mr. Jenkins, tell me something. What were you doing at that bus stop to begin with?"

"I was chillin'."

"By yourself?"

"Yeah."

"And you expect us to believe that?"

"I thought you said you'd come back tomorrow. Why are you still here, actin' suspicious? I'm the one who got stabbed. Someone attempted to murder me. Try and let that sink into ya'lls thick, prejudice skulls."

"Damon Jenkins!"

"Yes, Mama?"

"You better apologize to these kind officers, Damon? Damon!"

Mama Dukes was hollering my name because I'd closed my eyes, pretending to have suddenly fallen asleep. I snored loud enough to wake the entire hospital.

When I opened my eyes again, the popos were gone and Mama Dukes was eyeing me while shaking her head disdainfully.

"When will this ever end?" she asked, teary eyed. Why was she crying? I was far too weak to handle this much stress, this soon. I desperately needed my homeboys.

"Mama Dukes, where are my friends?" I asked with sudden dread. Nothing could prepare me for what she said next.

"You know," Mama Dukes replied, "the very next morning after you were admitted into the ICU, I began telling all of your friends that you died."

"Say what?" I asked, dazed from shock. "You did what?"

"I had to, son! Three days ago someone stabbed you and left you for dead at that bus stop. No tellin' what they would do next if they discovered you were still alive."

"But Ma, that ain't right."

"You know what's not right? All of this here. All these shady things that happen to you ain't right. Hangin' out at a bus stop that late at night with your godforsaken friends ain't right. Lyin' to the cops ain't right. The story you just told the police ain't right."

"It ain't no story, Ma, it's the truth."

"The same truth that shot Frank to death and left his body next to a dumpster near Sistrunk?"

"What? Frank got shot?"

"Frank got dead."

"My best friend is dead?"

"Sho' is."

"This don't even make sense," I mumbled, fighting back tears. The pain from the bad news pierced a hole inside my heart. If Frank was dead, it meant my other two homeboys were dead as well. Anonymous' name was written all over this. She'd murdered my friends to cover her ass.

It just had to be her.

"I bet the same person that stabbed you, gunned down your friends," Mama reasoned.

I eyed her with disgust. It was her fault. She told my homeboys I was dead. They in turn relay the message to Anonymous, who in turn set them up and had them killed in order to cover her tracks. I politely requested to be left alone. After Mama Dukes was gone, I closed my eyes and wept bitterly. My best friends were all dead.

Their names had been ringing in my head for three days now. *"Lexi, did any of these hoodlums hurt you? Stewart, help Lexi into the car."*

As soon as I recovered, I planned on locating and destroying Anonymous, her baldheaded man,

Stewart and of course, Lexi, the bitch who stabbed me.

CHAPTER FIVE
D-MONEY

Seven Months Later

It was 1:55 p.m. and the Saturday afternoon weather was a gloomy lookin' one. Despite the overcast, my spirits were indeed very high. I was sailing North on SR7 in Shug-B's play boy ride, boppin' my head to the beat of Jay-Z's 'On to the Next One'. I couldn't remember the last time I was this merry and here are my reasons why.

Firstly, I was rollin' in a hot ride; wasn't my ride, but nonetheless, it felt good rollin' it. Sistas wuz breakin' their necks trynna make out who was drivin' such hot ride, but failed miserably because the windows were up and Shug-B had done his tint real dark.

It seemed the cops no longer gave two cents about extra dark tints these days, and I was glad because dark tint added certain mystery to one's ride. Shug-B's spankin' new drop-top Mercedes Benz was on point and I had to force myself not to let the top down and draw too much attention to myself. I made a left onto 19th Street in Lauderhill, slowed down, and double-checked the GPS. Yeah, I was headed in the right direction.

My second reason for being in such high spirits wuz due to the easy $1,000.00 I would make within less than a few minutes on such a gloomy Saturday afternoon. Things sure seemed a lot scarier without my homeboys around, but, then again, rollin' alone would prolly work out better in the long run. Shit, three persons less meant three hundred percent less attention and three hundred percent increased agility. Regardless, my homeboys and I had never been caught, never been jailed because we knew our shit. So, attention and agility were both non-factors. Period. We were pros; and together, we were frickin' invincible.

There it was. I had finally arrived at my destination. I decelerated to about two miles per hour, and mentally scrutinized the area. There were two large garages on the west side of the street and a humongous gap between both garages. There was a lot going on in this gap. Several Jamaican men sat around tables smashin' dominoes; others, both men and women, were eating jerk chicken, drinking liquor, and checkin' out the awesome rides. I kept my windows up as I continued to observe people's body languages to ensure there were no cops or snitches in the area.

Over on the east side of the street was an open lot where a group of men stood smokin'. Seemed to me they were smokin' weed. A few of them were lookin' in my direction. I had no clue who I'd been sent here to see, which heightened my liking for the particular task at hand. What I didn't know couldn't hurt me. I ignored the goons in the open lot and redirected my focus to the garage area. Someone in the crowd waved a Jamaican flag. This was the cue I'd been lookin' for. It was time for me to exit the car and make the pick-up for Shug-B, deliver it to him, and collect my G—an easy one-two task that suddenly turned out to be quite the nightmare.

As I was about to exit the car, the sound of sirens infiltrated the air; within minutes police had the entire area surrounded. I remained in my vehicle as my heartbeat intensified. What the hell was going on? Had they been spyin' on me this whole time? How was that even possible? I could have sworn Shug-B and I had been careful.

I knew I couldn't risk bein' anywhere near a police bust, anytime soon. No tellin' what these cops were up to, dawg. I braced my balls and started the engine, because I now noticed all the focus was directed at the gathering in the garage side of the street. So my initial hypothesis was wrong. The cops had no idea I was here.

Apparently, no one had noticed me—yet. While the cops were barkin' out orders for people to remain where they were, I managed to make it to the end of the street before one of them shouted through a loudspeaker, "Stop your vehicle at once!" At this point, it was either do or die. I decided to keep goin'. I knew immediately that some of the cops had already commenced a chase. I darted past 21st Street ignoring all stop signs, veered onto 26th and shot towards SR7. Shug-B's ride was faster than a mofo. I could hear the sirens in the distance, gaining proximity. Moments later the fools were on my tail. I sailed through the red light at the intersection of 26th Street and SR7, swerved around oncoming traffic, ignored the honking of angry drivers as I gathered more speed towards Sunrise Blvd.

I quickly glanced at my rearview mirror and noticed the cop car that was closest to me had collided with a red Corolla. Another car had come to a halt, but two others circumvented the commotion and were closing in on me. Ignoring another red light at the intersection of Sunrise Blvd and SR7, I whizzed through oncoming traffic and headed east on Sunrise towards I-95. I affixed my eyes to the streets and reached sideways to retrieve the pre-paid phone that was chillin' on the passenger seat of my car. I glanced at my rearview again. The cops were about to close in on me. I floored the gas pedal and felt myself flying past the Swap Shop. My heart almost jumped from my chest. I eyed the side view mirrors. No sign of any police cars. I knew my victory would be short-lived because the sirens were getting louder. I-95. Finally. I swerved onto I-95 and continued north towards nowhere in particular.

"C'mon, pick up, pick up, pick up," I murmured, breathlessly, wonderin' if the car was outta breath too. Shit. I had to find somethin' to keep me from freakin' out and gettin' imprisoned.

"Talk to me," Shug-B said, reminding me of my homeboys that died. That's how they'd always answer their phones.

"Shug-B, shit! They're after me mehn. Tell me what to do, dawg!"

"D-Money?"

"Yeah, dawg, tell me quick! They 'bout to close in on me, mehn!"

"What the hell happened? Did you screw this up?"

"Let's talk about dat later, man, they about to be on my ass, dawg!"

"You think you could lose 'em?"

"Yeah, dawg!"

"Aight. Aight, lemme think for a second."

I eyed my rearview mirror and saw about ten police cars about a mile away. "C'mon Shug-B, think quick, dawg."

"Aight then, where you at now?"

"Headin' north on I-95, goin' over a hundred miles an hour. Next exit is Commercial."

"D', if I find out you blew my cover; if you screwed me over—"

"Naw, Shug, you know I'd never do no messed up crap like that, dawg! I'mma tell you e'rything I know. Just help me out of this mess!"

"Aight, see if you can exit off Copans. Go West. Make a right onto Powerline Road, and head north. Make a right at Sample, and head East. Make a right at 30th Avenue then pull into the apartment complex on the right. Exit the vehicle, give the keys to my 16 year old daughter and hide. She'll take it from there."

"Dang! You expect me to remember all that?"

"I'mma call my daughter and tell her to act like she was the one drivin' all along. Then I'mma gonna call the cops and tell 'em my car is missin'. Just pray that this shit works.

When I pulled into the apartment complex, Deidre was already waitin' for me as Shug-B had promised. I felt as if I could breathe again.

"Keys, please," she ordered, rolling her neck sista girl style. Oh hellz naw. "Keys, fool!" she shouted again.

The loud wail of sirens was upon us. Lame ass popos just wouldn't quit. I quickly dashed out of the vehicle and headed for the bushes. Deidre dashed inside of the vehicle and took off. Moments later police cars followed in pursuit of her.

I was out of a thousand dollars and I wasn't sure if Shug-B's plan would work. All I was sure of was that I was saved for the moment. And I needed to give this illegitimate way of life a break. It was time for me to find a new means of survival; well, at least for now, or until I figured out how I would seize Lexi.

CHAPTER SIX
D-MONEY

Five Months Later

First of all let me just say this: life is a bitch. It had already been about a year since my recovery, and I still felt like the cops had their eyes on my ass. I mean, you would think that I was the one who attempted to murder somebody at the bus stop that night and not the other way around. I could somewhat understand why they were always hounding me, but I couldn't see why no one even cared about my suffering. The cops didn't even try to find my assailant, let alone bring justice to the killer of my three homeboys. It's as if we didn't even count. But it was all good though. I knew exactly who my assailant was, I knew who murdered my homeboys, and I planned on being my own justice system.

I mean, my three friends were gunned down the day after I was stabbed and left for dead at a bus stop. That shit should at least count for somethin', but it didn't; I couldn't understand why not. But like I said, it's all good.

Anonymous. Stewart. Lexi. Bald-headed dude. Naw, Lexi would be the first on my list. She was the cause of awla this. If she hadn't wounded me so violently that night, my friends would still be alive today. Shit, I would still be alive, because as far as I'm concerned, I might as well have been dead. My boys are dead, all because of Lexi, and it was slowly killing me too.

I could no longer make moves and feel safe because they weren't here to have my back. They're all dead because of Lexi. The popos were now on my ass so much, I couldn't even fart properly if I tried. Things were tough, and getting' tougher. I needed money. I'd sold my purple Cadillac a few months back, but the funds from that sale were quickly running out and I was getting' hungry again, real fast. I wasn't used to bein' broke—well at least not like this. On top of all of that, my neighbors kept lookin' at me funny, and it was still extremely difficult adjusting to half of a colon. Yes. Lexi would have to die. I planned on makin' the others suffer, too; however, Lexi had now become my number one target. I was now willing to go to prison for killing this bitch.

I must say though, it all came to me as a surprise when one week ago, I received a call from Blew

Horizon's Cab Services. I could hardly believe I'd really landed the gig.

Mama Dukes was thrilled to know that I could finally state my job title without seemin' shady. She was convinced I was now turning my life around, and was even more pleased that my "godforsaken friends", according to her, were no longer around to lead me astray.

The old hag. If it hadn't been for all the times she had rescued me; been my alibi on several occasions, I would have busted a cap in her head. As far as I'm concerned, if she hadn't told my homeboys that I was dead, then Anonymous would have had no reason to feel the need to murder them in cold blood, in order to cover her ass. However, if Lexi hadn't stabbed me, Mama Dukes would have had no need to lie to my homeboys. It was all Lexi's fault.

Never before in my life had I ever spent so many hours workin' each day, for nickels and dimes. It took me five days to earn what my friends and I used to earn in thirty minutes.

I kept myself motivated by thinking less about the stingy wages. I thought of my job as a cover-up for my true motive. I needed everyone to think that I was now on the straight and narrow. Furthermore, I had no other means of getting' bread right now. Not with things the way they were. As a cab driver, I'd be able to hunt easily. I could stay mobile even though I no longer owned a car. I'd be able to get my revenge after all. Just the thought of that had me crunked.

There was something else that also kept me going. Lemme explain. I couldn't help but wonder often, whatever happened to the young lady who was tied up in the trunk of my car the night I got stabbed by Lexi? What in hell had my homeboys done with her? Maybe it's a good thing after all that they were all dead. This way, there ain't no witnesses, no snitches—no nothin'.

Furthermore, my friends and I were wearing leather gloves that night, so there were no fingerprints.

I still planned on avenging my friends' death, if it was the last thing I do in life.

CHAPTER SEVEN
D-MONEY

Two Years & Four Months Later

Strip joints are hot! I jumped into my cab, started the engine, and exited the premises of Bootylicious Babez, located off of Broward Blvd and Federal Highway. I attempted for the umpteenth time to wipe the smug grin from my face, but failed yet again. I could hardly blame myself though; I mean my smile was the result of spending one hundred dollars wisely and Juicy G' had just taught me the new meaning to the term 'good bang for the buck.'

I swung onto the main road and headed west on Broward Blvd. The announcement of a call offer jerked me from my pleasant thoughts. I immediately pushed the button to verify the location of the caller and quickly accepted the offer. I continued west on Broward and then made a left onto I-95 South. I was about to do a pick-up at the Fort Lauderdale Airport.

Given my now messed up life, today was, indeed, turning out to be a very good day so far. I was satisfied in more ways than one. It had been smooth sailing since my next customer was just around the corner and I'd possibly earn a good sum after completin' the trip.

My wild locks danced in the cool evening wind as I sailed down the highway towards the airport. My spirits were high. I adjusted the rearview mirror so I could eye my locks. The general manager of Blew Horizon's had encouraged me to get rid of them, so as not to scare away his customers. His encouragement sounded more like a warning though. Shit. Ain't no way I was going to get rid o' these fine ass locks! My eyes wandered from my locks to the ridiculous grin on my face. Dang! I was still grinning? My spirit must have been real high. My grin quickly dissipated upon the memory of over a month ago, which was the last time I'd been this happy. That shit ended up in a police chase.

Suddenly, I was angry again. I was angry at the fact that I couldn't trust my happiness. Every time I was happy, something ended up going wrong. For instance, I was happy hangin' with my homeboys; now my homeboys are all dead. How can I smile when they're dead, and the killer is still out there enjoyin' her fabulous life? I was happy about a month ago when I attempted to run that errand for Shug-B. That shit almost cost me my freedom and an opportunity to avenge my boys.

I slowed the vehicle as I approached the terminal of my destination. I wondered what the hell was about to go wrong. Something bad was 'bout to go down, 'cause that's the kinda shit that'd been happenin' to me. E'ry time I was in high spirits something terrible would go wrong.

I pulled up at Caribbean Express Airlines and observed the area. It didn't appear that anyone was awaiting my arrival. I was about to double-check the information I had previously received when I was suddenly startled by the sound of a huge bang coming from the back of the cab. Immediately, I felt myself jerking up and down as the cab shook. What the-?

I quickly turned around and that's when I noticed him. I quickly hopped outside of the vehicle so that I could get a much closer look. My eyes hadn't deceived me and I wasn't seeing doubles. He was that huge.

He banged on the trunk of the car again and I jumped from my thoughts.

"Yu want fi take a picture of me?" He asked sneeringly.

"Ain't nothin', man. Just wonderin' if you are Biggs," I replied. His arrogant shrug was my confirmation.

Within seconds the trunk was opened and the dude placed his belongings inside of it.

"You all set?" I asked, trynna play shit off.

"Me alright, mon," he replied in the heaviest Caribbean accent I'd ever heard in my entire life. He must have been born in the Bahamas or sumthin'.

I watched as he rolled towards the front of the vehicle and sat in the front passenger seat of the cab. Oh hell naw! Did he really plan on sittin' next to my ass? When there was a lot more space in the back? Oh hell naw! I wasn't about to sit side by side with this feisty kat, man. I got it now. He must be Jamaican. Jamaicans were the only passengers who sit in the front passenger seat of a cab. Did they think that shit was cute?

"Yo, bredrin? What yu waitin' for? Judgment? Get yu ass inside of this cab and start drivin' right now. Bloodclaut, mon!"

Oh, hellz naw, did this negro know who I was?

"Yo! Pussy! Come drive this; now!" he said.

Back in the day, me and my boys would kill for less than this. I bit my bottom lip and furrowed my brows in deep thought. I needed to decide what to do with this cocky bastard. I needed to teach him a lesson. I started the engine and rolled out of the airport wondering how I was gonna take this dude down—by myself. The ringing of a cell phone interrupted my thoughts.

"Yes, mon, me reach!" he answered.

"Yes, mon, no, mon," I mocked internally. I zoned in on his conversation so I could escape my imagination for a while, in an attempt to allow my evil thoughts to marinate.

"Yes, mon. The cab arrived," he continued.

I quickly ran through his credentials in my head. His name was Biggs. Well, that name surely did him justice.

"Anonymous, it wasn't my fault, mon. The plane flight was delayed."

I shook my head in utter wonderment. Not at the fact that Biggs' used the term 'plane flight'; but at the name he'd just uttered.

"But I neva said Nita. I called you Anonymous. How can anyone possibly know who you are by me callin' you A..."

Biggs froze in his seat next to me and my mind froze as well—well at least after I was done considering the probability of another woman, besides my ex-boss lady, actually going by the name of Anonymous. I mentally computed the probability to be equal to zero. Not even one in a million or any shit like that; just straight up zero. I, D'-Money Jenkins, therefore concluded that the bitch on the phone was the bitch who I now planned on hunting. And maybe she would lead me to this otha' bitch, Lexi. My mind had now become frozen after that thought. It was clear that the caller had disconnected the call, which was the typical behavior of this particular bourgeois brat I once knew and worked for. Very small world, indeed!

"Yo, verify your destination again, mehn," I requested as soon as words re-entered my thoughts. I remained in silence as he read the address that was scribbled on a sheet of paper. There was no need for me to take out this sucker yet. He was about to lead me to my second greatest enemy, Anonymous.

Like I said, the plan was now for Biggs to lead me to Anonymous, who would then lead me to Lexi, whether she liked the idea or not. Thing is, nothing could prepare me for what happened next.

After a few weeks of trailing him, Biggs' accomplice remained hidden. I'd done damn near everything, from shuffling my shift, to cutting my hours, but continued to fail miserably at my hunting endeavors.

I finally made the decision few weeks into my quest, to pounce on Biggs unawares, at his crib, and force him to help me lure Anonymous into my trap. But the day I showed up at his apartment complex and broke into his crib, I found Biggs sprawled out on the floor, covered in blood. Someone had gotten to him before I could. I eyed the leather gloves on my hands and reminisced on the good times I've had using them. My homeboys and I had matching sets of gloves, but now there were no more homeboys; no more good times; only more death and disappointments.

The sudden wails of approaching sirens jerked me from my thoughts. I wondered if someone, in what I'd considered to be a deserted neighborhood, had spotted me climb up to Biggs' house from the backside and onto the balcony. I briefly contemplated exiting through the front, but ended up darting through the back instead. It was a risk that I needed to take. After all, there was a dead man lying on the floor of unit 207; it was more probable that the popos were here to investigate that incident or somethin' related to it.

I successfully made it back to my cab that was parked on the opposite end of the parking lot, facing Bigg's apartment. A swat team headed upstairs while a team of FBI agents and police swarmed the area. Good thing I'd made my exit through the back. Dang, it seemed like cops were always showing up everywhere I go. Mama Dukes always warned me about stuff like that. You know—like signs. She always talked about Karma and sowing seeds. Was this all a sign that one day I would finally get caught and killed by the cops?

I remained in the distance and tried to observe the mayhem. My attention suddenly drifted to a very pretty white chick in a black pant suit, clearly FBI, walking across the parking lot. Her booty had caught my eyes. I ain't never seen a black girl's booty on a white girl before. I've seen it on 'em Latin chicks and Brazilian chicks. But not on no white chick.

The Caucasian lady moseyed her way to the east end of the parking lot and stopped at the window of a bright, blue Nissan Z. I hadn't noticed the car before. Couldn't even remember seeing it. Ms. Uh-Oh-Oreo shifted to the side revealing the face of the driver. I couldn't make out much of the driver from such a far distance, but I knew she was female.

Immediately, a number of questions came to mind, my number one being, "Who was the driver of the Nissan Z? Why was the FBI talking to her? Why was she even here?"

She was dark skin, so I knew it couldn't be Anonymous. Furthermore, Anonymous would have never showed up anywhere near a scene like this.

My imagination quickly began to run away with me. I was on the hunt for two women of opposite skin color. The first was Lexi, who had dark skin, while the second was Anonymous who was a red bone. The driver of the Z had dark skin.

I started the engine and pulled the cab out of parking. I made a right turn at the stop sign and another right turn at the stop sign after that one. I casually drove by the Z and got a better look at the two women who seemed deeply indulged in conversation. As I got closer, the woman in the driver's seat of the Z opened the car door and stepped outside of the car. My heart almost busted out of my chest upon my discovery. I rolled past the Z and out of Kascades. The driver of the Z was the woman who stabbed me. I floored the gas pedal and breathlessly breezed down 32nd Street. About a minute later I pulled over on a curb to get my head straight. I was pumped. I was ready to catch her and rip her apart. That was her. That had to be Lexi. Memories of the night at the bus stop flooded my thoughts, *"Lexi, did any of those hoodlums hurt you?"*

In that moment, I was sure. I had just positively ID'd the driver of the Nissan Z to be my assailant. *C'mon D'-Money! Think fast, think fast, think fast.*

My cell phone interrupted my thoughts. The caller ID announced that the General Manager of Blew Horizons was calling. I ignored the call. I hadn't accepted an offer all day. I spun the car around and headed in the direction from which I came.

As I approached 30th Street, I spotted the bright, blue Z pulling out of the Kascades, where Biggs had been staying.

I allowed a few cars ahead of me as cover. I headed towards Copans Road, made a left onto Sample Road, and continued west. I'd suddenly envisioned the ultimate punishment for Lexi.

Revenge was a dish best served cold. I eyed my leather gloves again and thought about my dead homeboys. My heart filled with pain. In order for my plan to work, I needed to exercise patience. I was now willing to wait for as long as it would take, to learn everything about her whereabouts, her family, her credentials. I planned on ripping the people she loved the most from her life as was done to me. I'd make her suffer before I killed her. I decided to spare her life for the time being. My inspiration for such a decision was due to the fact that she was pregnant. She stepped out of that Z, and didn't even realize she'd stepped into a death trap. She's endangered her life and that of her unborn child, by having stabbed me at the bus stop that night.

One day soon, when her child is old enough, I would strike, and rip him or her away from Lexi. Then I would rip her man away from her, and then I'd shred her to pieces. Mark my words; before these pages are through, you'll be a witness as I unleash my wrath upon Lexi and all that she loves.

pages are through, you'll be a witness as I unleash my wrath upon Lexi and all that she loves.

CHAPTER EIGHT
EVERHARD

Present Day (Jamaica)

"Rastafari!" I and I shouted gleefully as I and I skipped around the mango tree and flashed I mon locks flamboyantly. I and I wondered what my psychiatrist would do if she should see I mon right now. Yes, I have a psychiatrist and so what? Look at you. I'm sure that you could use one yourself, so don't judge Selassie's son.

Anyway, the things I and I am about to reveal will shock you.

Before I and I reveal anything to you, I will first stand underneath the Guangu tree in my backyard, and proudly admire my vegetable garden. The Callaloo I'd planted only a few weeks ago clustered healthily together in the Callaloo bed, showing off their vivid green to my bright red tomatoes that were situated on the opposite end of the garden. Mixed within this vegetation were my marijuana plants, but let's not discuss that right now. Selassie's son is beyond happy.

It wasn't just the lushness of I and I garden that made I mon so joyful; it was also the good news that I mon had heard a few weeks prior to this.

Bloodclaut, rasta! Everytime I and I thought about the good news, I mon couldn't help but shout out a bloodclaut or two.

Let I mon explain the runnings.

The long and short of it is basically this.

About six years ago, I was forcefully sodomized by my stepdaughter, Lexi. She and her hooligan friends had ganged up against I and I and unleashed upon I mon the most brutish, inhumane acts known to man. It's only by the mercy of Selassie that I mon lived. I won't even bother to get into the reason why she claimed she did it. The only thing you should know is that Lexi is an evil bitch.

No one, certainly not I, know for sure how she turned out to be so immoral, so corrupt, so evil! I and I don't even want to get into that. All I mon know is that, if Lexi knew what I had planned, she'd just kill herself before I got to her. So I am sure you can understand how happy I mon was when I and I learnt that I mon would be getting my American visa soon. Bomboclaut! Jah! Rastafari, he who liveth and ruleth the world! Tell I and I that that is not good news and I mon will prove you wrong!

This is how it happened.

It seemed that Lexi had crossed the wrong people when she'd travelled to America. One of the ladies she crossed ended up in prison, because of a testimony with which Lexi had furnished the court.

The empress who Lexi testified against is the daughter of Jeremy K. Styles, ex-Prime Minister of Jamaica. When Prime Minister Styles found out that Lexi had crossed his daughter, it immediately set him on a path of revenge.

He arrived at I mon's house a few weeks ago with his entourage; it had looked more like a motorcade in my front yard that day. Anyway, he wanted I and I to give him some news about Lexi: her family, her whereabouts—basically, her whole life. He told I mon that Lexi had fallen off the face of the earth some years ago, but was now back on the scene.

I told Mr. Styles I had no information about that evil bitch.

He implored me to dig deep and share whatever info I could, as his daughter had now been incarcerated and was no longer privy to the most up-to-date info regarding Lexi.

I and I immediately fit the pieces of the puzzle together and realized that Politician Styles was up to no good. He must have seen the expression on I mon's face and believe he was frightening me. But I mon wasn't frightened. I mon was actually glad.

"Everhard, or whatever you call yourself, I'm willing to buy you a ticket out of here if you cooperate with me," he said.

But shit, I might've cooperated with him for free; if he'd just waited a second later he would have seen me leap from my chair with excitement to know that someone influential possibly wanted Lexi dead. But he didn't, so I changed my mind. But I mon wasn't freaked out at all.

"Well, the most I mon know is that Lexi grew up with her grandparents, then later—"

"Yes, he interrupted, "we are already aware of the old folks; matter of fact, we have them."

"What you mean, you have them?"

"Don't worry about that. The mother. I understand that the mother has now relocated to the US as well?"

"Yu talking about Lexi's mother? Sonia?"

"Correct."

"Well, the last time I mon heard from the mother, was about six weeks ago. She said she was only calling I mon to remind I and I that I was a son of a bitch. She also bragged to I mon about her new husband."

"So she's now married?"

"That is what she tell I."

"Did she say where in the US she currently resides?"

"Resides?"

"Lives. Where in America does she live at the moment?"

"Oh! Yes, Sir I mean, no Sir. She didn't say where exactly."

"Alright. Is there anything else you can think of?"

"How soon can you get I mon that ticket out of here, Mr. Styles, Sir?"

"I will work something out and contact you soon."

"You'll contact I mon soon?"

"Precisely. Oh and another thing, do keep your mouth shut about this visit. Or you won't live long enough to regret it. Understand?" Mr. Styles said coolly.

"Yes, Mr. Styles. I, I mon understand you loud and clear."

"Very well then. Gentlemen, let's be on our way," He stood, addressing the two sturdily built young men that accompanied him. I meant to ask Mr. Styles what he meant when he stated that he had Lexi's grandparents, but I reconsidered. I mean really. Who gives a shit? Certainly not Selassie's son.

As far as I and I was concerned, it will certainly be my pleasure to personally relay the information to Lexi as soon as I arrived in America. I planned on doing some serious damage. Lexi will not know what hit her.

My only concern is that it had already been about three weeks and I still haven't heard from Prime Minister Styles.

A loud banging interrupted my thoughts. The sound was coming from the front of the house. Someone was at the front door. I mon heart skipped a beat at the thought of Minister Styles. Had he arrived with my visa? I and I was about to light up a spliff; however, a visa to America was much more important. The weed could wait.

I took one last glance at my vegetables and headed inside of the house. As I made my way inside, my mind wandered back to the visit I had from Minister Styles. Gwaan, Jah Jah! Show Babylon that your son is risin' from the valley of destruction!

I mon hadn't really heard from Mr. Styles since then. Better yet, he hadn't even contacted I mon once. Come to think of it, the whole thing seemed strange. I mean, I mon hadn't provided him with much information to go with, but I mon did the best I mon could. Furthermore, he promised me that damn visa. And who the hell had he threatened? Me? I and I? It had just registered just now, that that son-of-a-politician bitch had threatened Selassie's son. Who the hell did he think he was? Selassie? Fire pon him rass-claut!

As far as I mon was concerned, Lexi had single-handedly ripped I mon's life out of I mon's chest. My psychiatrist disagrees, but I more or less have nothing to live for. I mon's only motivation now was to exact revenge upon that crazy, heartless bitch. If that asshole politician didn't come through with his promise, I planned on taking the story to Carib News TV. And then after that-

A loud rap against my front door disrupted me from my thoughts again. I didn't even realize I'd reached the door and stood in front of it, spaced out. I wrapped my palms around the handle of the oversized door that screeched on its hinges as I pushed it forward.

"Everhard?" two police officers chorused, relieved to see me.

"Officer Briggadere and Officer Keith!" I greeted cordially. Both officers were popular within my vicinity.

"Everhard?" Officer Keith said.

"Yes?" I replied with a huge smile "did Styles send you with the visa?"

"Pardon?" Officer Keith replied, seeming a bit puzzled.

"Did Styles—"

"Hush up!" Officer Briggadere yelled impatiently, ordering me to be quiet.

"Keith, read this infidel his rights."

"Rights? What rights?"

"Everhard, ahem, Antonius Montique, I am placing you under arrest for the murder of Pollymae and Radclif Jones, Lexi Jones' grandparents. You have the right to remain—"

"Bloodclaut, Babylon bwoy! Let I mon go!"

"You have the right to remain silent. Anything—"

"Bomboclaut! I mon neva kill nuhbody! Tek off the cuffs offa Selassie son!"

"Anything you say or do can be used against you in a court of law."

And just like that, Babylon lock up I mon rass. Choh, bloodclaat.

CHAPTER NINE
LEXI

I licked my lips as I sashayed sultrily across the bedroom floor. My destination was my naked, delectable, hunk of a husband who stood at the opposite end of the room, mesmerized by my beauty.

I retrieved the shiny, black, leather whip from its holding place on waste and flicked my wrist, sending a gratifying crack across the room. I observed as a minute smile softened the intensity of his lustful expression.

"You've been a bad boy and I'm gonna teach you a lesson," I purred.

I took one final step, closing the gap between us, pulled him into me and slowly gyrated against his lower abdomen.

"Are you ready for your punishment?" I whispered hungrily into his ears.

"Give it to me," he replied, breathless from desire.

"Not so fast," I replied, pushing him face down onto the bed, and whipping him across his butt several times.

"I've learnt my lesson!" he wailed moments later, his submission enticing me.

"Turn over!" I ordered. He obeyed, looking up at me with big brown eyes and a devilish grin.

"You like that, huh?" I said, "gimme your hands."

I dropped the whip and retrieved the blindfold and handcuffs from my 'treasure chest'—if you know what I mean. I climbed atop my husband and restrained him by cuffing each of his wrists to the head-board and then I blindfolded him. I licked my index finger and gently grazed it over his nipples and down his chest. He writhed in anticipation.

"Baby," he moaned.

"Yes?" I purred.

"Sit on top of me?"

"Not yet."

I observed as his ample stiffness beckoned to me.

"Well hello to you, too," I said, greeting JT's vigorous erection. I traced my tongue, just my tongue, up and down his shaft. He moaned. I shifted my focus from his Johnson and bit his nipples.

"Oh, baby!" he said, writhing uncontrollably as I teased him. For a brief moment I considered using my nipple clamps, but it was only a thought. I didn't wish to spring too much upon JT too soon. I smiled at that thought.

"Baby, I just need you on top of me for twenty minutes, please?" he pleaded.

"Hmm, tell you what. I'm going to remove the blindfold so you can watch me dance for you."

"Shhhhit" he murmured, biting his lips.

I removed the blindfold and stared into his eyes as I climbed down from the bed, my movements slow and seductive.

"Allow me to remove these on your behalf," I said, motioning at my sinful, leather underwear.

I squeezed my nipples and massaged my breasts that were accentuated by my cupless merry widow. I twirled my hips slowly from side to side. A groan escaped JT's lips as he took me in. Still jiving, I turned my back towards him and swept my hair up with one hand, while using my other hand to pull against the strap of my shiny, black g-string. I then quickly let go of the strap allowing it to slap against my skin.

I let go of my hair, and smoothly transitioned into the 'Ben Dover' position, bending over at the waist, with legs spread apart, and ass propped up in the air, exposing the wealth of my center. I reached around and pulled on my garter strap, then let go, allowing it to slap against my skin. I fluidly shifted my g-string to the side for the big reveal. JT moaned again.

I want you now, he murmured, licking his lips and wining his waste in unison with my gyration. His massive erection reached out and touched me, and I knew I had to bring the torture to a close.

I undid my underwear—garters and all, climbed atop JT's muscular body once again, and took him inside of my hot, wet mouth. I allowed my tongue and upper palate to worship his anatomy. He groaned with gratifying delight.

"That's it, baby. That's it right there, oh-oh-shhh-oh," he moaned wildly.

I closed my eyes and hummed on his joystick. He cursed. I bobbed my head up and down my husband's dick, with plans of taking him where no other woman had ever taken him before. And this was just the beginning.

CHAPTER TEN
UNCLE DESMOND

I was visiting Jamaica to tie up a few loose ends before returning to my home in Florida for good, when things quickly spiraled out of control.
I had suddenly been involuntarily hurled into the midst of some serious 'Lexi drama', and at the moment was still incapable of overcoming the shock.

Let me start from the beginning. Several years ago, maybe eight or nine, my niece, Lexi, was entrusted to me by her grandparents, with whom she'd lived. I'd brought her to America to live with me, thus providing her with a new start. For reasons I'm unwilling to discuss at the moment, due to regret and being pressed for time, Lexi ended up leaving my home in the middle of the night only after a few months living at my home. What can I say? It is what it is. Sometimes things just don't work out the way we planned them.

I haven't heard from Lexi since then; and her mother and grandparents had completely turned against me. But let me not digress.

Five years ago, Lexi seemed to have been the target of every American news station. She'd become involved with one of the biggest real estate scandals to ever hit the globe. I devotedly followed the story, and even spent years after that seeking out Lexi, but to no avail. It had been made quite clear that she wanted nothing to do with the likes of me, so I gave up.

After Lexi had left my home, it seemed as if everything started to go wrong. First, the most stunning woman appeared out of nowhere and literally threw herself on me. She called herself Anonymous. As we warmed up to each other, she started asking me questions about Lexi, well not Lexi per se, just questions about my niece or children, etc. But as I'm fitting the pieces together, I now realize who Anonymous really is, and why she had shown up at my gate, so many years ago. But I'll get to that shortly. After spending intimate times together, Anonymous suddenly disappeared from my life- nearly broke my heart. But I recovered quickly.

Later, that same year, I was involved in a devastating car crash, which totaled my car and injured my spine. I ended up receiving a tidy sum from the insurance company and phenomenal medical care; however, my injury prevented me from performing up to par at my job and I was fired.

Now, several years later, I had to consider surviving my joblessness, injured spine, and a sunken economy. My last resort was to rent the home I owned in Manchester, Jamaica. The one in which my estranged wife currently resided. About a year ago when I'd brought up the idea to her, she'd dismissed me rudely.

She brought to my attention the fact that I hadn't made one mortgage payment in the last five years, and that she had taken over from where I'd left off, all these years.

So, I brought to her attention, the fact that her name was NOT on the deed, and I needed her to vacate the premises immediately.

I hadn't been able to get a hold of her since then, so two weeks ago, I returned to Jamaica to find out was going on. I visited my property, only to learn that Margaret, my estranged wife, had already rented out the property, and moved to Mandeville to live with her lover.

I had been spending the past few weeks since then, switching landlordship over to me, so that the tenant who currently occupied MY property, would pay rent to me, instead of idiot Margaret, hence the loose ends I'd been tying up. But things suddenly got out of hand. Before I explain how things got out of hand, let me first explain why.

Like I was saying earlier, some years ago, a strange woman showed up at my yard gate- strange, only because she was a stranger, because she was the hottest thing since pepper sauce. Anyway, to cut a long story short, she'd appeared at my home pretending to need help. So I helped her. She introduced herself to me as Anonymous, and slept with me to gather intel on Lexi's past. From what I learnt, Anonymous is the daughter of Politician Styles, ex-Prime Minister of Jamaica. Politician Styles finally learnt the truth surrounding his daughter's misfortune, and that it was Lexi's testimony that had helped sealed the deal regarding his daughter's incarceration. Heartbroken and outraged, Politician Styles has set out to get his revenge against Lexi, wreak havoc upon anyone who dare stand in his way.

A few days ago, when the rent for MY property had become due, and Margaret had gotten wind of my endeavors to release her from land lordship, she showed up at the property with Bunnie, her lover. She began yelling out obscenities, and said things such as:

"I hope you know that the property belongs to this man right here!" she pointed to Bunnie, "Bunnie is the man who's been paying your mortgage all these years, you son-of-a-bitch!"

Bunnie approached me, and was all up in my face. We were ready to throw down, when all of sudden, a white mini bus pulled up at the gate. Several men, masked in handkerchiefs, pounced upon us with guns, and escorted us all, including my tenant into the bus.

We were man-handled, tied up, blindfolded and carried to an unfinished concrete house, at an unidentified location deep into the woodlands. Hence my reason for saying things had spiraled way out of control. But the situation gets even worst.

A day ago when my blindfold was removed, I was devastated to see Lexi's grandparents, laid out across the dirt floor in front of me. Dead.

CHAPTER ELEVEN
LEXI

My husband, JT is a hardworking man, and an excellent father to our five-year-old son. We've been best friends since childhood, and I know that he'll always have my back, no matter what.

JT is gorgeous. His handsome face and chiseled features have scored him plenty of beautiful women; whose dreams of hitching him have been shattered by him. Because, even though he possesses the qualities I've just mentioned, he is also extremely self-centered.

JT doesn't know that I feel this way about him. In fact, although we've been best friends nearly all our lives, there's a lot of things my husband doesn't know about me, and the way I view things.

My son Lexington, named after me, is the most important person in my life. I put my son before myself; but after putting up with being JT's baby-momma and wife for over five years, I've decided that the wisest thing for me to do in this day and age, when men like JT were scarce, is to lock him down for good. After-all, we're already married, and have a beautiful son together.

Our marriage is a complicated one. As a matter of fact, I broke up with my boyfriend at the time, to marry JT- but that's a long story. What I will share though, is that my boyfriend Vaughnn Gibbs and I were madly in love, but had quickly become enemies before the wedding.

Most would say that JT ruined my love life. But I try to view things more positively. We have a comfortable life and a beautiful son together. JT and I have worked very hard to achieve the American dream.

I mean- I didn't have to work very hard when I was with Vaughnn. There was no 'building life' with him. Life was already built because he was already rich; but where has that gotten him? He was now imprisoned- so where's the life in that? I have come to the realization that everything really does happen for a reason. Hence my positive view on the life I have with JT.

I must say though, that I believe I died inside when Vaughnn and I broke up. The day I lost him, I died inside, but quickly found life again once Lexington was born. I'm not very sure where my marriage to JT is headed, but I figured the best thing to do when you have no control over certain situations, is to try and take life one day at a time.

I know you're wondering, so I'm just gonna say it. JT and I have an open marriage. However, it's only open for his benefit. My desire is to be with one man only, preferably the one to whom I was married.

Furthermore, I've always put my son first. He's always been my pride and joy, so I care very little to date men other than my husband.

The only issue was that now I desired the full package- just as much as the next woman. I now wanted my marriage to be exclusive. I wanted more out of my marriage, instead of just "taking it one day at a time", so I intended to close its doors.

Shit- every other woman was falling over their heels to be with JT, why shouldn't I do the same? I was definitely beginning to see things differently; plus, I-wasn't-getting-any-younger. Also, what about my son? He needed the stability of both parents. It was time for me to up my game. I needed to rock JT's world, and I planned on doing just that.

I had been taking our marriage for granted all these years, so now I needed to do something, and fast. I'd be foolish to let a man like JT slip from the palm of my hands. I wasn't about to just let him go like that. I wish I'd been thinking like this a lot sooner. JT and I deserved a shot at making our marriage work. For good. Exclusively.

With all the women who were after him, I knew I had my work cut out for me. However, I was already wifey. I was already the woman on the inside, so I could pull all the strings, and win.

CHAPTER TWELVE
JT

"Lexi, you are trippin'," I gazed with awe upon my wife's nakedness.

She had put our son to bed, and slipped into her birthday suit, an outfit that instantly reminded me of why I'd ended up giving her a son in the first place.

I shifted about awkwardly so as to properly position my unruly manhood.

"Are you gonna just stand over there and stare at me?"

I got up and walked towards my wife, admiring her beauty while restraining myself from jumping her guns right then. She kissed me gently on my lips. "That's better," she said sultrily, and then kissed me again. Heat rushed through my veins, igniting every organ within me. I pulled her small waistline into me so she could feel the hardness of my sizable member, and remember what sex with me was like.

"Lexi, it's been a while since we- are you sure you—"

"JT, don't be ridiculous," she whispered between kisses, cutting me off. "I bore you a son. Remember?"

I allowed her to undress me. Now we both stood naked, admiring each other. She ran her soft palms over my chest, and then gently sucked my nipples, one after the other.

"Such sexy abs," she mumbled beneath her breath as she continued to suck on a nipple while using the tip of her index finger to play with the other. I swear the nerves in my nipples were directly connected to the ones in my johnson. Her movements were making me so hard that not being inside of her was uncomfortable. I resisted the urge to throw her down on the floor and take her without abandon. It had been years since we'd been intimate.

I turned and took a few steps backward until I was leaned up against the wall. I needed the extra support for my now weakened limbs. Lexi was right there with me. Without missing a beat, she hungrily licked my lips, sucked my earlobes, and stuck her tongue down each of my ears. I closed my eyes and moaned uncontrollably. She positioned herself behind me, while rubbing her full breasts and soft skin against my body. A second later she was licking the back of my neck.

She rolled her tongue southward to the base of my spine, kissed my butt cheeks while gently fondling my stiffness.

I switched my position to the opposite wall, pressing both of my palms against it, in an attempt to balance my weight on my hands. Each movement for me was difficult because Lexi was all over me like a rabbit in heat. Her skillful tongue and fingers drove me to the peak of frenzy.

"I want you," I huffed.

"No, not yet," she gently nibbled on my jewels, before using her tongue to write tiny love letters on my love-rod.

"Lexi, come here," I said breathlessly. I watched as her bright, glossy eyes stared up into mine. She smiled. "Not yet."

I inhaled deeply, flexing my biceps in an attempt to remain standing. Lexi's tongue moved cleverly down the back of my leg and nestled in my underknee.

"Oh. My. God!" I gasped.

She moved to the next leg, and repeated the act. On her knees, she spun me around and kissed every inch of the areas surrounding my python.

I could hardly take it. Her teases were eliciting my mind-numbing need to have her- to be inside of her. Just as I was about to collapse, she took me inside of her mouth and sucked me. My heart exploded a million times.

She ran her tongue along my shaft, lapping up my sweet 'n low.

"Hmm, tasty," she murmured, licking her lips. She took me deep inside her throat once again, and hummed. Once again, I was breathless.

Her exploration induced the most mind-numbing orgasm ever.

She swallowed the product of her sultry exploits, and then licked up any remains.

I kneeled before her, bursting with satisfaction.

"Lie on your back and spread your legs. It's now your turn," I pointed to the ground. She obeyed.

Her skills and creativity had inspired me. I began to kiss and caress her, in a similar way she did me, targeting her breasts first. I licked the tips of her nipples, while cupping her moist center. She moaned.

I then traced my tongue down her abdomen and suckled on her belly button. She moaned again.

I kissed between her narrow waistline, and curvaceous hips. I was rattled by the anticipation of spreading those hips.

I rubbed my cheeks against the softness of her thick thighs.

Finally I parted her legs, revealing her plump, freshly waxed mound. I admired the pretty, pink spot from which her juices flowed, and licked it all up. She wailed in ecstasy. I licked her juicy center again and again, sporadically brushing my nose against her love button. Her moans heightened, as essence gushed from her honey pot.

"Damn girl! You're so wet- and so damn sexy," I looked up from my dining purlieu, and observed her as she writhed about.

With both her legs apart, she sat up, balancing on her elbows as she threw her head back, closed her eyes and suck in air between clenched teeth.

I lifted her leg and placed it over my shoulder as I trailed my tongue along her thighs, down her calves, then back up again, burrowing my tongue within her underknee. Curses escaped her lips.
My tongue travelled north between her thighs and once again, mingled with her lush lips.

I nibbled lightly on her succulence and dismissed all hangups I had about my wife. In this moment, she was perfect.

No longer could I bear my desires to ravish her. I raised my body atop hers, kept her feet on my shoulders, and slid inside her.

Her muscles latched onto me as my rigid shaft fervently entered her tight walls. She dug her nails into my back. I leaned over and plunged my tongue into her mouth and down her throat as our lips locked.

I buried myself deeper and deeper inside of her. She clung to me as my thrusts intensified.

Her sex was so damn priceless.

I sucked her breasts as we moved our hips together.

I lamented amidst her cries and my moans.

She gyrated beneath me, her movements matching mine as we rocked rhythmically to the beat of music, only we could hear. We clung desperately to each other as we powerfully exploded. Together.

Motionless, we remained on the ground in silence. A silence that was suddenly broken by the cries of our son.

"I want mommy!" he cried.

"I think is heading this way," I said grabbing my pants. Lexi giggled as she remained naked on the carpet. I put on my pants just in time to catch Lexington before he entered the room.

"There he is!" I chuckled, "What happened little man? Did you have a nightmare?"

"I want my mommy!"

"Uh- your mommy is asleep, big guy" I said as I lifted him into my arms and carried him upstairs to his room.

"No she's not."

"Then where is she?"

"I don't know. You tell me."

"I just did. Alright, tell you what, I'll read you a bedtime story and then I'll look for mommy. How does that sound?"

"The Cat in the Hat!"

"Ok, Lex Jr., I'll read you the cat in the hat." By the time I was through reading the story, my son had fallen asleep. Lexi met me at his door. I smiled as I hugged and kissed her.

"Is he asleep?"

"Yup."

"Are you ready to go to sleep?" She smirked at me.

"Nope," I kept kissing her all over.

"Then- what do you wanna do?" She asked.

"Shower,"

"Go ahead. Let me know when you're done."

I chuckled and lifted her into my arms as I'd done my son previously.

"Oh, I won't need to," I said and headed towards the bathroom with her in my arms.

CHAPTER THIRTEEN
UNCLE DESMOND

As I came to, I could hear my captors bickering about what to do with me- with us. I attempted to open my eyes, but found the task impossible. My eyes felt too heavy. I assumed they were too swollen from the beating I'd received from the three men who'd been determined to obtain information from me, regarding the whereabouts of Lexi's mother, Sonia. I wondered why I felt so weak. I mean- I'd been badly beaten, but that alone couldn't have possibly accounted for my diluted state. Speaking of dilute, why the hell was I so wet? Warm liquid ran down my skull and over my forehead. It began to drip from my lashes and nose tip. The scent of my own blood horrified me. Was I really soaking in my own blood?

As pain steadily penetrated my core, I willed myself to remain conscious. The lapse in my memory alerted me that I'd drifted out of consciousness at least twice, and there was no telling I'd be so lucky as to awaken a third time. If this was my condition, what had happened to my wife Margaret, and her husband? And what about my tenant? Last, but definitely not least, what about my mother and father, Lexi's grandparents? I know I never mentioned it, nor ever acted like it, but they were my parents. They'd been brutally murdered, and I probably wouldn't even live to provide them a proper burial. It hurt too much to cry. I pushed all morbid thoughts to the back of my head. I didn't really know what was happening to me- couldn't remember as my pain clouded my memory. However, I needed to at least try to remain focused for the time being.

I remained steady and zoned in on the conversation.

"Benji- you are a bloodclaut fool. Why yu shoot all of dem, before getting the information for Politician Styles?"

"Because dem piss me off to rassclaut! Why dem acting like bomboclaut fools, everytime me ask dem about idiot Sonia? Dem pretending not to know where Sonia is."

"But it wasn't your call fi shoot dem, star. Now all of dem dead."

"Not all of dem."

"Yes, Benji. All of dem dead to pussy. Now what we gwine to do? Styles said he already have intel on Lexi and her likkle bwoy, and her man. All he need now is information on her mother. But you killed everybody who had that information."

"Not everybody dead!"

"What you mean?"

"Dat one still alive!"

"Which one?"

"Dat one!"

For a brief moment, there was complete silence. I knew they were referring to me. My heart pounded.

"No, mon. Him dead, mon."

"Benji! Cox! Blingers! Come now!" A fourth voice shouted from outside.

"Yo, Vader! You talk to Styles 'bout this?" one of my attackers yelled back.

"Yeah mon! Styles said it's all good. But we should hurry because him have another assignment for us! Let's go, this one is hot, hot," Vader's voice sounded much closer now. "You sure they all dead?" he asked.

"You mean they don't look dead enough to you?" someone else asked.

"Kiss mi neck-back! Benji, yuh really fuck dem up. Alright guys, oonu bounce wid me. Hurry!"

Within moments, there was complete silence. But I didn't trust such silence. I remained flat on my back, and succeeded in opening one eye, just enough to see the hardened expression of Benji, as he stood over me with a gun pointed at my head. He was going to finish me off for sure.

"Benji, what the fuck! Fire that gun one more time and I personally shoot up yuh bloodclaut!"

"This man nuh dead!"

"To rahtid! Why you so trigger happy? Look at all those dead bodies on the ground, and yuh still not satisfied? Let's get the hell out of here, now!"

So that was it. I'd been beaten and shot. I waited for two of the longest minutes of my life, and forced myself up. I could barely see through all the blood that dripped from my cracked skull. My swollen eyes didn't help much either. But the sight before me was more than I could bear.

Margaret? Margaret! Mama! Papa! Lloy! Bunnie! No response. I wept. I was dying and I knew it. But I needed to live so I could warn Lexi, and bury my parents. Our parents. It was now my only means of paying homage. I'd done a lot of wrong- too much wrong in my life. I needed to live so I could correct at least these two things.

I knew how these things worked. These murders would revisit the crime scene soon. If I was to survive, I needed to get out of there soon. I dragged myself out in the open, and looked around. I was in the middle of nowhere, surrounded by woods. I spotted an 8-foot, fallen bamboo, two feet away, and dragged myself towards it.

It was a miracle that I was still alive, given my significant blood loss, thus far. I fetched the bamboo, and used it for support in scrambling to my feet. I fought through the pain, and dragged my injured body in the direction of the tire tracks. I hoped that I didn't bleed to death, or that guardians of such a gruesome site wouldn't spot and kill me before I bled to death.

An hour later I was still dragging on and wondered how I'd remained alive. My mind wandered back to all the good food I'd eaten as a kid growing up in Jamaica. I reminisced about the many soft juicy apples and sweet East Indian mangoes I'd picked from the trees in my backyard. I recalled papa's lush vegetable field of callaloo, tomatoes, dasheen, yellow yams and gungo peas; mama's chicken coop that was always filled with healthy, naturally fed fowls. Growing up on authentic, whole, Jamaican foods must have been my source of strength, in a deadly situation such as this.

I smiled to myself at my silliness. Food couldn't have been the only reason. I mean- if that was the case, Margaret would have survived too. And believe me, Margaret was a very healthy looking woman, who knew how to throw down some vigorous

Jamaican cooking. My heart sank at the memory of her lifeless body. Two minutes later, my feet gave way and I stumbled to the ground on top of the bamboo.

I'd made a gruesome mistake. I'd been travelling in the direction of the tire tracks, and had stumbled in the way for the murderers to get a hold of me and finish me off. I considered rolling off into the side bushes. But it was far too late. I heard a vehicle coming. Furthermore, the blood trail I'd unwittingly left behind would soon be the end of me. As far as I was concerned, I was already a dead man. I could no longer endure. So I gave up. The sound of chattering grew louder, as the vehicle neared. Wasn't sure which direction the sound was coming from. But I was sure I'd delivered myself back into the hands of my enemies. I fainted.

CHAPTER FOURTEEN
JT

As I pulled up into my driveway I noticed an unfamiliar car parked behind my wife's BMW. Puzzled, I parked my Mercedes Benz next to my wife's car, shut off the engine, retrieved the gift from the passenger seat, and then got out of the car. I looked at my watch; it was a little past 3 pm and I knew my wife would not be expecting me home this early. My early arrival was a spontaneous one- and up until a minute ago when I noticed the white Escalade parked so presumptuously in my driveway, I greatly anticipated the reaction on my wife's and son's faces.

"Hmm," I thought to myself, while checking out the vehicle. Something about it was setting off alarms in my head, but I couldn't quite put my finger on what it was that I found so strange about the car, so I brushed the feeling, concluding that I had nothing to worry about.

Gift, still in my hand, I leaned back on my car and admired my townhome. I nodded with approval as I thought about how great my life had turned out to be. I'm still drop-dead gorgeous, I get any woman I want, I have the coolest wife ever, and I have excellent credit. Most dearest to me is my five year old son, Lexington, the most precious gift God could have ever blessed me with. Every day I give thanks for my son. I know a lot of people right now who would give anything to be in my shoes. Take for instance, my homeboy Kevin. Not a day goes by when he doesn't remind me of my lifestyle. Though people's comments about me and my success make me feel proud of who I am, I find it rather disturbing that they continue to probe and make inquiries regarding my personal life. They wonder how I maintain my lifestyle. It's almost as if they believe I do not deserve my success.

I shook my head, took one last look at the Escalade and then headed inside.

Upon entering the living-room, I couldn't believe my eyes. I was stunned by what I saw.

The shock of it had me suddenly overwhelmed. In panic I jumped, sending the gift bag I carried flying over my head, with its contents shattering on the floor. With that went the Chanel perfume I had gotten for my wife.

"What the hell!" I stared in horror at the scene before me.

"Lexi," I said, turning to my wife, "Can you explain what's going on here?"

"On the contrary," said my wife, "It is I who need an explanation from you."

"What the hell!" I repeated, suddenly at a loss for words. My wife continued to eye me smugly.

"Chill out and have a seat, JT," she rose from the sofa. "Sit down."

I sat down with my brows furrowed; a million thoughts racing through my mind. I tried to decipher the situation. I needed to figure out my next move.

"This lovely young lady came here to see you," my wife said, "What's your name again, hun?" she asked our visitor.

"Wendy," our visitor replied.

"Yes. Wendy. JT, your girlfriend Wendy came here today to check up on you," Lexi replied coolly, before turning away.

"Lexi, where are you going?" I asked my wife.

"To the kitchen," she said matter-of-factly, before disappearing.

I slowly turned my head towards Wendy, and through gritted teeth spoke, "What. Are. You. Doing. Here?"

"Why. Have. You. Been. Ignoring. My. Calls?" she mocked.

"Get your ass out of my house," I growled as I jumped up angrily from my seat and grabbed Wendy's arm.

"Stop acting like this," she said, blocking my attempts to lead her outside. I didn't care. I dragged her by the arm towards the front door, and into the driveway.

"How could you be so devious?" I was livid.

"Devious? I beg to differ."

"Why did you come here? My home is sacred to me. I never gave you permission to come to my home. Sitting in my living-room, talking to my wife? Are you freaking retarded?"

"Retarded? JT, really?"

"Why the hell would you show up here and disrespect my family—my wife?"

"Disrespect your family? JT! You disrespect your family all by yourself. You're the one who's cheating on your wife, remember?"

"Wendy, I made it clear to you. Respect my boundaries and we're good. What happened to our little agreement? Huh?"

"What did you expect? I've been calling and calling and calling-"

"Then leave a message! Isn't that what a voicemail is for?"

"I have left you several messages, you pig. You never replied. Don't think I'm just gonna sit back and allow you to get away with using me."

"Using you? Don't you dare try me, Wendy! My wife is inside-"

"JT, I'm your woman-"

"Excuse me? Have you forgotten I am a married man?"

"Screw your marriage! You don't care about her. Have you forgotten the things you 've told me?"

"Wendy, are you threatening me?"

"No. I'm reminding you, asshole. Acting like you have some sort of god-complex or something. I'm only here because you promised that you'd go with me to buy the Escalade we were looking at together. You could have at least called to check up on me- see if I'd gotten the car, but-"

"Go home, Wendy," I said, cutting her off. I eyed the brand new Escalade that was parked next to my wife's BMW, and thought about Vaughnn, the man who was now imprisoned, because Lexi had testified against him in court five years ago. He drove a vehicle similar to that.

"JT, I'm in love with you—"

"Get home, Wendy."

"I'm sorry- I just wanted—"

"Go-home-Wendy," I repeated, cutting her off again. I didn't wish to hear her bullshit. She had crossed the line and I was pissed off as hell.

I didn't wait to hear another word from her. I stormed inside the house, and slammed my door behind me. I was quickly beginning to realize that Wendy's madness knew no bounds. I couldn't even begin to fathom how she'd found out where I lived. I mean- she knew nothing about my wife- that my wife's insanity quadrupled hers.

What if she'd received a different reaction from my Lexi? I mean- Wendy wasn't aware of the details of my marriage. Speaking of, why the hell had Lexi been so damn collected about the whole situation? What the hell was she up to now?

Wendy is nothing but a crazy-ass bitch. I mean- if I knew she was this insane- I would have left her ass alone. It's a pity that—

"That was fast," my wife suddenly reappeared into the living room.

"What was?" I observed her fluid movements as she set the dinner table.

"You got rid of her in record speed," she replied, smiling smugly.

"Lexi, I'm sorry about that. I don't even know how she found out where I live."

"I was surprised when she showed up at the door. I figured it would be interesting to have her wait for you," Lexi said, still smiling.

"Interesting? How long had she been waiting?" I asked, puzzled. I'd been married to Lexi for over five years now, but no matter how hard I tried, I couldn't trust her. No telling when she would strike again, as she's done in the past.

"She really hadn't been waiting for that long- maybe twenty minutes, or so. Matter-of-fact, when you showed up here early, I assumed you knew she was here."

"What? Are you crazy? I always tell these women, my home and family is my life and sanctuary. I warn them to stay away—"

"Well- clearly your little rule did not apply to this chick."

"Clearly," I chuckled. I eyed Lexi as she slipped back into the kitchen and returned with a pitcher of passion fruit juice.

All of her movements were skilled. Especially in the bedroom. She winked at me and smiled. Her smile was gorgeous. She was beautiful, her body was on point. But she wasn't enough for me. As a matter of fact, I'd come home early to discuss getting a divorce. The Chanel perfume was to cushion the blow. But that was water under the bridge now, as its remnants were now on the floor, courtesy of Wendy, my side chick. Or should I say my ex-side-chick. Didn't matter though, I would be asking Lexi for a divorce, whether she liked it or not. After-all, I now had everything I needed; and she had everything she needed. I'd grown weary of her. It was time for us to call it quits. I so desperately yearned for freedom- especially from my crazy ass wife.

"JT, do you let your women know that I only married you so you can get your green-card?" she asked thoughtfully.

"So it's like that?"

"I'm serious. Do you?"

"I do- but most don't believe me."

"Why not?"

"I guess it's mostly because we have a son together."

"Oh. Wow."

"Why, wow?"

"If your women don't believe you, then they must be thinking that I'm a damn fool."

"Why?"

"Because I married a man who openly cheats on me."

"Since when did you start caring about what people think?"

"Actually- I've been thinking about it for a while. I'm also thinking that that's the reason your little girlfriend thought it a good idea to show up at our home. JT- how do you expect I would feel about that?"

"I'm so sorry about that- I really am, but Lexi, when did you start caring about people's perception of you?"

"Excuse me?"

"I don't mean it like that. I'm just sayin' you never gave a damn what people think."

"So I should just sit back and accept disrespect?"

"Of course not. Listen, how long have you felt this way?"

"I've always felt like this."

"I actually had no idea."

"Yeah, you know you've got to right your wrong."

"Meaning what?"

"JT, don't you think I'm drop dead gorgeous?"

"You know you're mad sexy-"

"I know I'm mad sexy, but do you?" She sashayed across the living room, and sat in the chair facing me.

I placed my gaze on the floor.

"JT, look at me."

I removed my gaze from the floor, briefly glanced at her boobs— briefly, then returned my gaze to the floor.

"JT!"

"Ok! Lexi, yes. I think you're stunning."

"Then what's the problem?"

"What's the problem with what?"

"What's the problem with us?"

"There's no problem with us; we're good."

"No we're not."

"Lexi, why are you trippin' right now?"

"I don't think that I'm trippin'. I'm just merely pointing out the obvious."

"Which is?"

"You have a stunning wife, who is your best friend, and also the mother of your child."

"Lexi, what are you getting at?" She now had my full attention, and I was staring her dead in the eyes. I hoped this wasn't what I thought. I've waited too long for this, and I wasn't about to be coerced into eternal marriage with my wife. No way. I had too many plans- too much to look forward to. My entire future depended completely breaking away from Lexi. I wanted a divorce as soon as possible.

"JT, we've been married for a while now, right?"

"You want a divorce?" I asked, cutting her off. I was excited that she'd been the one to bring up the subject. *Freedom at last!*

"Actually, quite the opposite," she paused and my heart sank.

"Lexi, what are you saying?" I wanted to pinch myself to see if I was having a nightmare.

"I'm saying that we share a son together. My ex-boyfriend, Vaughnn is safely tucked away in prison, and according to you, can no longer harm us, plus we've been married for all these years."

"So?' I asked, now fearful of her response.

"I say we make this official."

"Make what official?" I asked, hoping to the bitter end that I was really having a nightmare.

"I say we make our marriage official. Let us honor our wedding vows, and make our relationship exclusive?"

"Uh-huh."

"JT?"

I didn't know what the fuck Lexi was saying right now. I didn't feel like hearing that shit. My mind wandered back to Jamaica, my island home. Back to the days when I was free of Lexi, free of marriage, free of all of this mess.

"JT!" Lexi said, her tone now sounding a bit more rigid.

" Are you actually serious?" I asked, in hopes that she would answer no.

"Yes," she answered, to my grave disappointment. "You're damn right I'm serious."

"Oh."

"JT, you're supposed to be my best friend. Why are you so hesitant about being with me? Has the past six years been so bad?"

"I didn't say that."

"Then what's the big deal? I know you find me attractive. Plus you know that I'm a damn good mother to our son— our son, JT. What more could you possibly want in a woman?"

I don't know. How about sanity for starters?

"Are you still with me?"

"I'm still with you."

"So, what are your thoughts right now?"

"Hmm," I replied thoughtfully, "Why don't we give this some thought?"

"I already have. Now I need your thoughts on this."

Once again, I was stuck between a rock and a hard spot. It would seem like complete betrayal if I should disappoint her; we were supposed to be best friends. In my mind however, America had changed all of that. Life had changed all of that. No longer had I even considered Lexi my best friend.

"I've been living a certain lifestyle for all these years; a lifestyle you've been privy to. I'm sure it's reasonable for me to ask for some more time to think about your proposition."

"You really need more time to think about this?" Lexi asked in astonishment.

"Just to make sure that this is what we both want," I replied, attempting to cushion the blow of my response.

"Well, ok then I guess," she struggled to hide her disappointment. "I've already thought about this. So if you need more time, take it. Just don't take too much time. We've already wasted enough time already."

"Do you mean that you have already wasted enough time?"

"Even so, I need your answer soon."

"I promise I'll give this some thought and get back to you soon. I won't waste anymore of your time," I assured her, but I really wasn't quite so sure at all.

I knew, however, that staying married to Lexi was the last thing I intended to do. I already constructed my post-divorce initiative, which included Lexi as only my baby-momma.

"A promise is a comfort to a fool," she whispered into my ears before scampering off to the kitchen. It's almost as if she could read my mind.

"JT!" she shouted.

"Yes!"

"Please clean up the mess you made out front."

"You mean the Chanel perfume I got you?"

"That's Chanel? See, now your bitch owes me!"

Ignoring her comment, I sighed in frustration and wondered if this day could possibly get any worse. I retrieved the cell phone from my pocket. It had been vibrating since I slammed the door in Wendy's face.

I stared at my cell phone, puzzled. I briefly wondered who could be calling me from a blocked number, and shook my head in disgust as I considered Wendy. As I was about to answer the call, a huge rock came crashing through the glass window. It landed on the glass center piece in front of me, smashing it to smithereens. In response I quickly used my elbows to block shards and splinters from blinding me and ruining my face. The phone fell from my hands onto the floor. Moments later Lexi appeared inside the living-room—flabbergasted.

CHAPTER FIFTEEN
LEXI

I chased inside the living room to see what the commotion was, and was horror-struck by the scene before me.

JT was barely a couple paces away from where the rock had landed.

"What was that?" I whispered, horrified. "Are you hurt?"

"Lexi, get down!" he'd barely finished his sentence when another smashed through the same window as before. It landed on the seat where I was, only moments prior, when I was speaking with my husband.

"JT, what the hell!" I was horrified.

"JT, come out here bitch!" a female shouted from outside.

JT and I glanced at each other, bewildered. By this time we were both on the ground, on all fours.

"Do you hear me punk? Get your ass out here and face me like a man," the female challenged.

"JT, who is that?" I asked, bewildered.

He broke our gaze and sighed heavily, "It's Wendy."

"Who?" I asked.

"Wendy. It's Wendy."

"You mean the woman who was here a little while ago?"

"Yes." He jumped up and raced towards the door. I got up and rushed towards the safest corner of the living room. I needed to be able to witness the shit that was going down inside my home, between JT and his bitch.

JT had already disappeared outside, I presumed to drive away the crazy heifer.

"Remove yourself from my property or I will call the police."

"You're a pussy!"

"Wendy!"

"Go ahead! Call the cops, jackass. I'll wait until you're done and tell your precious wife all the nasty things you've been saying about her!"

Things? What things? This woman was delusional. What could JT have possibly told her about me, for her to use it as ammunition against him? Nothing, that's what. JT and I had been best friends for years. He would never discuss me or our marriage with anyone. He was done talking to her for sure. There was no doubt in my mind that he was on his way inside to call the police. I mean, what if my son had been home playing. He would have possible gotten seriously hurt. Yes. My husband was through reasoning with this psycopath.

"Wendy, why are you doing this?"

"Did you really think you could just use me and lose me—asshole? Did you?"

Was I hearing right? Was my husband still outside negotiating with that woman?

"Do not throw that—Wendy, do not throw that rock!"

"Fuck you!"

"Are you really serious right now? There are children living in this neighborhood-"

"Fuck 'em!"

"Watch your filthy mouth! Just be a woman and walk away. Alright? You and I are over. Done. Finished!"

"My ass! It's not over until the fat lady fucks you up! Did you tell your wife how much you can't stand her?"

"Leave my property!"

"You know what? I know exactly what to do. Watch your back, bitch!"

Moments later, her wheels skidded on the road, as she apparently sailed out of our neighborhood.

CHAPTER SIXTEEN
LEXI

"Did she just threaten you?" I asked, shocked and confused.

"I had no idea she was this crazy," he entered the house without stopping to address me.

"Are you going to call the cops?"

"Yes," he headed towards the house phone.

"Are you gonna tell me what that was about?"

"What do you mean? You just saw what happened."

"Is any of the things she said true? JT, have you been telling your women horrible things about me?"

"Jesus! Lexi, don't you know me by now? I would never discuss you or our relationship with anyone at all, let alone the women I sleep with."

As I moved towards JT, something buzzed against my heel. I looked down and saw that is cell phone was on the ground. Dodging glass fragments, I retrieved the phone from the floor. The call had been blocked.

"Someone's call your phone unidentified.

"It's her! It's that psycho again. She's been calling me unknown all evening. Let me see this."

He replaced the house phone back on its receiver. I handed him his phone, still completely shaken by the situation at hand.

"Shouldn't you be calling the cops?" I was flustered. Why wouldn't he speak to me? What was going on? Who was this Wendy heifer?

"She has kids—"

"She just committed a crime against our household, and you're worried about hers?"

"Lexi, she's not thinking straight right now, and-"

"Get out of my way, I'll call the fucking cops myself," I breezed past him and grabbed the house phone. I was livid.

As I was about to dial 911, JT began speaking on his cell.

"Hello," he answered. The horror reflected on his face urged me to replace the phone. Nothing could have prepared me for what happened next.

CHAPTER SEVENTEEN
JT

"Hello," I answered. There was silence on the other end of the line.

"Hello, Wendy, I know it's you," I was enraged.

"This ain't no got-dang Wendy. Does this sound like Wendy to you snitch?" a gruff voice returned.

My heart began to race as fear consumed me. For the past five years, I'd been expecting a phone call such as this one.

"Give the phone to your wife!" the caller demanded. I stood where I was, frozen.

"Did you hear me, punk? I said give the phone to your wife!"

"Wh-who is this?" I stuttered, finally finding the courage to speak.

"First name Kharma, last name, your-worst-nightmare! How has the last five years been?"

"If y-you don't tell me who you are and wh-why you're calling, I'm going to hang up the phone and call the police."

"Call the police and I'll blow your skull to pieces. Now, from this point forward, you're gonna do as I say. Give the phone to your wife. You have thirty seconds to get her on the phone."

"JT, what the hell is going on-" Lexi's voice trailed off as she studied my look of horror.

"Shhh," I whispered, as I muted the cell phone. I was confused as hell. I didn't know what to do next. Should I cover for Lexi? Or should I do as I'd been told and hand her over to the unknown caller? My family meant the world to me. My five year old Lexington was my life.

"What's going on?" Lexi whispered.

"I think our past has come back to haunt us."

"What do you mean?"

"I think that Vaughnn is after us."

"What? But it's been five years since-"

"Somebody wants to talk to you; he said I had thirty seconds to put you on-"

"Gimme this!" Lexi said, grabbing the phone from my palm.

"Who is this and what do you want?" she asked.

Her expression slowly mirrored mine as she listened to the caller.

"Listen to me, you son-of-a-bitch! If you call this number again, I will..." Lexi paused as if she'd been interrupted by the brusque caller. She remained silent for another minute or two. Shit, it could have been five. Then she disconnected the call.

"What did that fool say to you, Lexi?"

"JT, I think we're being stalked."

"By whom? Why? What did he say to you?"

"He told me that soon we'll need a new sitter."

"You mean baby-sitter?"

"Yes, JT. Someone has been stalking us, he even mentioned Lexington's name, his favorite toy, favorite game."

"I'm calling the police."

"You can't do that," Lexi said.

"Why not, Lexi? You're obviously in shock. Someone wants to harm our five year old son, and you want me to keep my mouth shut?"

"I'm trying to save our lives."

"Lexi, what did that man say to you?"

"Sit down, let me talk to you."

CHAPTER EIGHTEEN
LEXI

"Sit down, let me talk to you," I said to Vaughnn dismally, staring out into nothingness. He joined me on the loveseat; the look of terror in his eyes mirrored mine. The phone call I'd received was most disturbing. I'd just been threatened by an unknown caller. Based on the threats I realized my family and I had been ensnared. There was no way out of this mess. Whoever it is that was after us was already several steps ahead. How could I look my husband in the eyes and explain to him just how fucked we were? Oh, god! Lexington.

"My son! I need my son!" I cried. I reached over the sofa handle and hastily grabbed the phone from its receiver.

I dialed my babysitter's number and waited for her to answer. It was Friday. Carlecia usually took my Lexington of Thursdays and returned him to us on Friday afternoons. It was a thing between her and my son. Lexington adored Carlecia.

There was no answer. Was my son safe? I dialed Carlecia's phone number again, wondering how the hell the caller had obtained JT's cell number.

C'mon, c'mon, pick up, pick up…

"Mommy!" Lexington screamed with glee, chasing towards me as soon as he entered the living room.

"Lex?" I gasped with relief. Telephone still in my hand.

"We're back," Carlecia announced animatedly as she entered the room.

"Lexi, talk to me. Why shouldn't I call the police?" my husband asked.

"Shhh!" I said, shushing him. "Not in front of our son."

I embraced my son lovingly as he dived into my arms. "My sweet, sweet son," I said, kissing him on his cherry cheeks.

"May I help you?" Carlecia said, again animated. She was answering my call. I didn't even realize the home phone was still in my hand. I had just dialed her phone number when she and my son entered the house.

"Oh, my bad," I said, forcing a smile and disconnecting the call.

"Didn't expect us back so soon?" Carlecia asked chirpily.

"No. I actually didn't," I replied, handing the phone to Lexi.

"Mommy, Carlecia said that I was muddy and she bathed me."

"Awww, isn't Carlecia the nicest sitter ever? Huh? Huh?"

"No! She looked at my willy."

"Come over here and let me see if your little willy still has mud on it," Carlecia giggled.

"My willy is not little!" Lexington disputed. "Daddy, tell Carlecia what you said. You said that we have big balls!"

"That's right! C'mon, put it here for daddy," JT said, leaning over to pop fists with our son. The display was priceless.

"You see, Carlecia? Daddy said I have big balls!"

"You tell her," I said, placing him to stand on the floor.

"I'm going upstairs to check if my willy got bigger!" he screamed, chasing upstairs to his room.

I struggled to hold back tears. In six short days, all of this would be over. Soon we would all be killed. My precious innocent son, who's never hurt a fly, would be paying a brutal price for the sins of my past. Who was to be blamed for that?

"Are you kidding me, JT? Is that what you're teaching your son?" Carlecia quipped.

"What do you know about anything? You're just the sitter," JT snapped.

"Aren't we a bit testy today," Carlecia replied, suddenly turning around to leave. I was embarrassed for her. What JT had said was completely uncalled for.

"Lexi, you can pay me next week after my trip to Orlando."

"Hold up; you're leaving already?"

"Let that bitch go," JT snarled.

"Excuse me?" Carlecia asked, turning back around to face us.

"Excuse yourself."

"JT!" I said in an attempt to rein back in his rudeness.

"I don't need to put up with you," our sitter said bitterly, now completely focused on JT.

"Then don't. Bounce. Peace," JT replied.

"JT, how can you say that when you know her life might be in danger?"

"Her man can protect her. Ain't that right, idiot Carlecia?" JT asked.

Was I really hearing what I thought I was hearing? I was being completely ignored. The sexual tension between my husband and babysitter was so thick, I could reach out and cut it into slices. Was this for real? My husband and my sitter? No way.

I'd given up so much for the son-of-a-bitch that sat next to me in the sofa, yet his passion for Carlecia, our son's sitter, clearly outweighed his passion for me. By far. Of all the women that JT could have selected, he chose to be with my sitter? I glimpsed a hint of tears in her eyes before she stormed out of our home. I was angry. Only moments ago JT expressed his feelings against disrespecting Lexington and me, by bringing some tramp into our home. While, all the while he'd been screwing Carlecia, our son's sitter, right under my nose.

How could I have missed that? I wondered what the bitch was thinking all those times when I left her alone with JT and my son. I considered all the trips I made to Maryland to visit my mother, leaving JT behind with the sitter. I considered all the good-loving and energy I had been wasting on this arrogant, selfish son-of-a-bitch, and allowed my heart to rip into pieces.

It finally hit me. For the first time in our many years of friendship, I actually felt used by him. JT had used and betrayed me, just as my step father had done when I was a child.

Hurt, flustered and confused, I closed my eyes, traced my palm over my face, and then rubbed my temples. What a day this had turned out to be? I comforted my heart with thoughts of my son. I needed to do everything I could to protect Lexington, even if it cost me my life. Informing the police of the death threats I'd received, was completely out of the picture. Yet it seemed to be the only idea JT had. He wasn't even man enough to protect his home; his son. He's never been man enough. For several years, since our marriage, I had been the one wearing the pants in our relationship. JT don't run this. I do.

"Are you gonna tell me what's going on?" he scowled. He seemed more upset at Carlecia than he was at the fact that a hit was out on our lives.

I sighed deeply, cleaned my throat, and spoke.

"We cannot call the police."

"Bullshit! Lexi, our lives-"

"If we go to the cops, he'll put a bullet through our son's head. He said he'll kill all of us; even our sitter."

I paused for a moment to observe his reaction. He shifted awkwardly in the sofa before finally standing. Was he more concerned about Carlecia than he was about his family? I was numb. I thought I'd already been through my share of tribulations in life. I thought I deserved a shot of complete happiness. But I guess I thought wrong. I was hurt and terrified, and that shit wasn't cool. I placed my heartache on the backburner, so I could focus on a matter of more significance; and that is, saving my son's life.

"Lexi, answer me!"

"Huh? What?"

"The caller, what else did he tell you?"

"He said that we had approximately six days to live. A day for each year I'd taken away from his life. He explained that at the end of day six, you, Lexington and I would be taken and made to suffer extensively until we wished for death. He warned that our every movement was being tailed, and it would be to our benefit to make use of the six days with which we have been gifted."

"Lexi, we have to call the police—"

"JT, have you suddenly gone mad? The police are definitely out of it—"

"What about Ms. Cartright?"

"We cannot notify the FBI—"

"But the FBI is already involved—"

"JT, you can't be sure that it's Vaughnn who's threatening us. Furthermore, wouldn't this be a situation for the police to handle? And we cannot contact the police."

"If we contacted the police, how would they know? How would anyone know, if we explain the situation to the cops. Plus, it wouldn't hurt to contact Ms. Cartright—"

"It wouldn't hurt for you to keep your mouth shut."

"Lexi—"

"JT, that's enough."

"No, it's not enough. You know what? Maybe we don't have to call the cops ourselves; maybe the neighbors have already called the cops after Wendy's ruckus."

"So what? If the cops show up here we still cannot mention anything to do with the phone threats."

"Lexi!"

"JT! This day has all of a sudden become so bizarre and scary. I'm going upstairs to be with my son."

CHAPTER NINETEEN
LEXI

Upstairs, in his bedroom, my son seated me on his blue beanbag and placed a toy gun in my hand.

"Mommy, are you mad at daddy?" he asked, busying himself around the room.

"I'm kind of mad at him, but we'll be okay," I said, placing the toy gun on the floor next to me, while envying my son's energy.

"No, mommy, don't!" Lexington shouted, plunging forward to retrieve the toy gun, placing it back into my palm. "Mommy, you keep this for your protection."

"Protection from what, honey?" I asked, astonished. Lex held his head down and refused to meet my gaze.

"Lex, what should I do with the gun?" I asked, my horror proliferating by the second. I feared the worst. I feared that my son was suggesting violence against his own father. What kind of child was this? What kind of child had I raised? Where did my son—
"

"I will guard the door. If the bad men come for you, I will finish them," my son replied, racing towards his room door.

"W- what bad men honey?" I asked my son, even more confused and horrified.

"The ones that are coming for you and daddy."

"Lex, where did you hear that?" I asked, as my heart pounded. My son looked at me with bright brown eyes, but didn't respond. I rose from the beanbag and slowly walked towards him.

"C'mon, honey, talk to mommy. Who told you that there were bad men coming to get your mommy and daddy?"

"Am I gonna get in trouble?"

"No, sweetheart. You talk to your mommy. Tell mommy where you got your information.

"Information?"

"Yes, baby, who told you about the bad men?"

"When I was at Carlecia's playing football in the yard with Jimmy—"

"What happened when you were playing with Jimmy, honey?" I gulped. I gently wiped invisible sweat from my son's forehead and coerced him to speak.

"C'mon, talk to your mommy. I promise not to tell."

"You promise?"

"I promise, honey. Cross my heart." I bit my lips in grave anticipation, wishing I could calm my heartbeat; wishing I could negate my fear.

"It was my turn to get the ball. I ran to the yard gate to pick it up, and that's when I saw him," Lexington explained.

"S- see who honey?" I gulped again.

"The man in the black car."

"What man? What did he do? What did he say to you?"

"He told me that he was gonna kill my parents."

"Oh, Lex," I gasped, fighting tears and more horror. What kind of coward would threaten a five year old child? I inhaled deeply and kissed my son's cherry cheeks. Would Vaughnn really have done that? Would he really have stooped so low as to send those cowards to threaten a small child? Who was after me?

"That man is a coward. Nobody can kill us, do you hear me?"

Lex nodded innocently.

"Your mommy is not gonna die. In fact, I'll make sure that this bad man never comes near you again. Ok?"

My son nodded again. I hugged him. I loved my son so much. Despite my horrendous childhood, I'd turned out to be a wonderful mother. So far.

"Did you tell Carlecia about this?" I asked.

"Nope."

"Did you tell Jimmy, or anyone else?"

"Nope," my son shook his head.

"Ok, honey," I said, standing, "the man in the black car is a moron. Don't you ever, ever speak to strangers. Do you hear me? Remember what daddy taught you?"

"Yes, mommy."

"Ok, good. Now show me some karate moves," I said, sniffing back tears.

"Jimmy can't do this move better than me," my son said. He stood with his arms stretched out on each side, while bringing one knee up towards his waste and kicking frontward, while counting each kick, "Ichi! Ni! San! Shi! Roko! Shichi! Hachi! Ku! Ju!"

"Wicked!" I said, praising my son absentmindedly. "Show me some other moves."

Heart racing, I returned to my seat on the beanbag.

"He-aw! Did you see that move, mommy? Mommy, did you see that?"

"That was another wicked move, honey. Is that the side kick?"

"No, this is the side kick," my son demonstrated his move.

My son must be so traumatized. As soon as this was all over I planned on taking him to see a professional—a shrink or something, to have my son reset. Now that he'd become distracted with his moves from Karate class, I could use the time to think. I wiped beads of sweat from my forehead as I attempted to gather my thoughts. The thought of strangers traumatizing my son left a deep hollow within me.

My cell phone rang. I retrieved it from the pocket of my cargo shorts. The caller ID announced an unfamiliar phone number. The area code was 1-876. Someone was calling from Jamaica. Grandma! Grandpa!

"Hello," I answered eager to speak with my grandparents. They were the only two people on this planet, besides my son, that had never failed me. Seemed there'd be no room for joy, but there was. Speaking to my loving grandparents would be the highlight of my day.

"Lexi, how are you?" the caller replied, in a rather strained tone.

"Grandpa, are you alright?" I asked, puzzled. I hoped that he was alright. After all, this day couldn't possibly get any worst.

"Lexi, I'm calling you from the Mandeville hospital."

"Hospital? Grandpa, what's wrong? Oh, my god!"

"Lexi, this is not your grandfather. Please calm down and listen to me carefully."

"Who is this?" I asked, frustrated.

"This is your Uncle Desmond, Lexi. I've been admitted into the Mandeville hospital in critical condition, but I have something important to tell you. Please don't hang up on—"

I disconnected the call. How dare he call my number? That son-of-a-bitch. I took another deep breath, relieved that it wasn't grandpa that was in the ICU. Good. At least my grandparents were alright. I'd give them a call as soon as I figured out a way to escape my current predicament.

My son was running about kicking, cart-wheeling, shouting, just having a grand time in his own little world that was free of troubles.

It was good that Uncle Desmond was suffering. Nice of him to call and let me know that. Karma really was a bitch. In life, we hardly ever get to actually see our enemies suffer. The fact that Desmond called to let me know that he was reaping the seeds he'd sown, had suddenly lifted my mood— helped me to focus.

I thought about Vaughnn. Who else but Vaughnn could be after me? I then considered all the people I'd crossed in the past.

First, there was that man I'd stabbed at the bus stop, about eight years ago when he and his friends tried to rape me. I never really gave it much thought, but, had I killed him? Was he dead? And whatever happened to his three friends? Could they be the ones hunting me down? My husband had a friend who crossed him. Biggs.

While living in Jamaica, my husband's closest friend, Biggs, double-crossed him, and was later found murdered in his Pompano Beach apartment. How he'd obtained a visa to visit America, remained a mystery to JT and me. If Biggs could get the miraculous opportunity to travel to America, then so could my stepfather, Everhard. I'd unleashed my wrath on that bastard, and I know he despises me for what I'd done to him. Was it Everhard that was after me?

Then there were Vaughnn's associates to consider—all the men who had gone to prison because of my testimony five years ago.

I had considered Bonita as well.

See, Bonita, nicknamed Anonymous, was a very close friend of Vaughnn. Back in the day, she took it real personal when Vaughnn and I fell in love. She became jealous, and consistently plotted against me. Several years later when I sold Vaughnn out to the FBI, she was caught in the middle, and was now incarcerated. Bonita was never a match for me; especially now that she was imprisoned.

Shit, my enemies were many. As far as I knew, it could be anyone, or any number of criminals that was after me and my family.

All roads no longer led to Vaughnn. That thought scared me even more. I realized that my pursuers were much farther than just a few steps ahead of me. They were miles and miles ahead. How would I escape this?

Five years ago, after Vaughnn was imprisoned, the FBI assured me that no stones had been left unturned, and Vaughnn's men had all been scooped up. So, could he really be a part of this? This was all so crazy. How could I not have prepared myself; protected myself better?

Getting involved with Vaughnn had been a huge mistake, but remaining in South Florida with my family, was definitely an even bigger one.

The strange caller had mentioned a few things that made me suspect he was working for Vaughnn, or one of Vaughnn's comrades. He'd called me a snitch and he'd used the words 'five' and 'years' in the same sentence. Whoever was behind this, had taken a whole five years to organize this attack against my family and I.

The unidentified caller had also mentioned intimate details about my son, which meant that my home was possibly under surveillance. My telephones were bugged. Even as I sat here with my son, I was possibly being monitored by several persons. Several, because it would take several men to carry out the plan that had been partially revealed to me by the unidentified caller.

The enemy was, indeed, many, many steps ahead of me; however, just like six years ago, I was being underestimated.

The enemy had chosen the wrong woman to mess with. They had traumatized the wrong woman's child; threatened the wrong woman's family. I was Lexi Jones, dammit. What my pursuers failed to realize was that, I could be similar to them if I needed to. The kind of blood that ran through their veins, was the same kind that ran through mine.

I planned on using whatever means necessary to protect and defend myself, and the people I loved. No way would I go down without putting up a solid fight. If Vaughnn or any of his associates wanted me dead, they would have to escape prison first, hunt me down personally, and kill me themselves.

Let the damn games begin!

CHAPTER TWENTY
LEXI

I retrieved the gift-box from my 'treasure chest', and removed from it, my pocket pistol and silencer. Approximately eight years ago I stabbed a man with my butcher knife and left him for dead at a bus stop. If he and his friends had minded their own business and left me alone, I wouldn't have fucked him up. I wondered what ever happened to his friends after that. I smiled to myself at the memory of Vaughnn and Stewart, rushing to my rescue that night.

My relationship with Vaughnn had been perfect. He'd taken such good care of me and protected me from his ex-girlfriend's schemes.

The weapon in my hand was a gift from Vaughnn eight years ago when he was, according to Stewart, upgrading me from my butcher knife. My god, the love of my life had now become my worst enemy. And Stewart. Whatever happened to Stewart, and his brothers? They and Vaughnn had been so closely knit. It seemed they'd completely fallen off of the globe. I was glad however, that

Stewart and his brothers had still not been located by the authorities.

As I placed the weapon in my pocket book and packed a weekend bag for my son, my mind wandered to my mother. Her life was now in danger. I hadn't heard from her in weeks, which now terrified me. How long had my family been under surveillance? Had they located my mother and her new husband and harmed them? I was desperate to call mom, but didn't want to put her at risk, in case they hadn't gotten to her as yet.

I inhaled deeply and prayed for mom to be alright. I also prayed for her to not call, providing she was alright. This was truly a predicament. I'd become paranoid as hell. However, it was my paranoia that would possibly end up saving all of our lives.

My mind wandered back to the man I stabbed at the bus stop. I reflected on the butcher knife I had used on him. Vaughnn might have upgraded me from butcher knife to pistol, but over the years I still found it necessary to keep my butcher knife safe. Right now it was tucked away in the garage. It would be nice to retrieve it and carry it around in my boots- just in case.

I fled down the stairs, through the kitchen hall, and into the garage, which was already open. In my haste I tumbled over the gas pail which had been sitting in the walk area. I fell on my knees and elbows and bruised myself. Fucking gas pail! It hurt so much.

JT entered the room, saw that I was hurt, but ignored me. My knees were bleeding. Dammit. I hurled myself up, kicked the gas pail, and returned inside the house to clean myself up. It didn't even make sense. I'd gone into the garage to retrieve my knife, injured myself via the stupid gas pail, and ended up not getting the knife. I was in so much pain. Screw the gas pail and screw the butcher knife.

As I cleaned myself up, I thought about my situation. I was trying to look at things from all angles now—putting myself in my pursuers' shoes and thinking like them.

When I was a child, my mother and her man, Everhard, betrayed me. It was a miracle that I'd forgiven my mother's betrayal, but forgiving her had brought much peace to my life. I ended up getting a visa for her and invited her to live with my family and I in America. Her life had changed tremendously, and continued to change after she met Tyrese Nembhard a little over two years ago, while we were all visiting Miami Beach.

We later learnt that Tyrese was an affluent entrepreneur who owned several car washes in Maryland. He was here in Florida on vacation and had become smitten with my mom. Mom ended up moving to Maryland with him, where they tied the knot seven months ago.

Not hearing from mom for three weeks didn't really come as a surprise to me though; I knew Tyrese had been keeping her busy these days. After-all, they were madly in love, and still young and hot, so why not? I trusted that they were both alright. Plus, I was about to make my move, and in order for it to work, Tyrese and my mom would have to be alright. If they weren't, I was screwed. Then again, I was already screwed to begin with, since Vaughnn's helpers had me cornered in the worst kind of way.

Regardless of my dilemma, I was about to set the only plan I had, in motion; and check up on mother, as soon as the way was clear. For right now, I dared not focus on the possibility of her being harmed.

I had finished packing the weekend bag for my son; I had my weapon in place, along with a plan. All I needed now was to take a few more minutes to mentally go over the details and iron out the rough edges.

I headed downstairs and spotted JT pacing about in the den. Jackass. I still wasn't sure how to feel about him. So I placed my thoughts of him in a tickler file in the back of my mind, and exited the house.

I strolled to my mailbox in deep thought. Those fuckers were probably watching me right now; clocking my every movement. I suddenly wondered why they had given us six days. Yeah. Why had they given us six days? They'd obviously been stalking us for a while now, so why choose now to come out of the shadows and give us a timeline, instead of killing us? Something didn't add up.

It's almost as if they were waiting for something, but what? Were they waiting for me to make a certain move? Why put so much effort into plans of seizing my family, and then risk it all by attracting needless attention? I say 'they', because I've given things some serious thought and now know for sure that my family is being hunted by several persons who are following Vaughnn's directives.

I pushed those thoughts aside as well. This was obviously a part of their little game; a part of the torture. They had us where they wanted us, and would stop at nothing to make our lives a living hell.

I opened my mailbox and collected the mail that had arrived. Bills, bills, and more bills. Shit. In America, bills arrive before they are due. As soon as you got rid of one, another pops up.

I could see clearly now. It was imperative that I executed my plan.

As I headed back inside, I noticed a letter I'd accidentally overlooked. It had my name on it, but no address or stamp. It's as if someone, other than the mail man had placed it directly into my mailbox. This was strange.

I entered the living-room, placed the bills in the mail-holder, and continued to study the strange looking envelope. What in the world could this be now? More shit?

I was already on serious overload; there wasn't much more that I could take.

I rushed upstairs to my bedroom and grabbed the items I'd put together. I placed the envelope in my pocket book and then returned to my son's room, and took his hand.

"Hey baby," I greeted him with a smile, "look at how much you've sweat."

"You see my sweat mommy? You see how I can sweat just like daddy, when he's working out?"

"Yes. My son is becoming quite the man," I praised, as I led Lexington downstairs.

"Are we going somewhere mommy?"

"Yes, we are."

"Yay! Is daddy coming with us?"

"Lexi, are you going somewhere?" JT asked as he approached me, out of nowhere. He'd been running about the house like the coward that he was. When had my husband become such a coward? The JT I knew back in the day was the most fearless man I'd ever met. What could have possibly softened him up so much?

"I'm taking Lex to his play date," I said, winking at him.

"What play date?" my husband asked, clueless. "Our son doesn't—"

"Ok, see you in a little bit then?" I said cutting him off. I headed out the door with my son, and left JT behind, dumbfounded. I didn't wish to deal with, or think about JT right now.

"Lexi!" he shouted from behind. "Where are you taking my son?"

See? That's the kind of shit JT did to piss me off. Why was he creating a scene, knowing full well that there were gun men spying on us?

"Honey, let me drop Lex off at his play date, so we can have some time to ourselves. Ok?" I shouted. Hoping the bastards could hear me, wherever they were.

As I pulled out of my driveway, and onto the street, I eyed my son lovingly through the rearview mirror, and quickly dismissed thoughts of reconsidering the move I was about to make.

There was nothing extravagant about my next move. I had a gut feeling and intended to act on it immediately. The move I was about to make was completely unanticipated, and would therefore work in my favor for the time being.

Everything else I would play by air.

CHAPTER TWENTY ONE
LEXI

I merged onto I-75 S, travelled for about two miles and then exited on Pines Blvd. I eyed my rearview mirror to check on my son. He seemed completely preoccupied with his PlayStation Portable. I glanced at both side-view mirrors and tried to observe the behavior of the traffic behind me.

I continued directly onto Pines Blvd. and then made a left onto North Flamingo Road. That's when I noticed the black Pontiac five cars behind. The Pontiac was the only car that had seemed suspicious. It also matched the description my son had given. I kept my eyes on the Pontiac and made a right turn. Moments later, the number of cars behind me dwindled to two, but suddenly out of nowhere, a white cab entered the scene. There was plenty of traffic space ahead of me, yet, all three cars remained behind me.

I passed the Pembroke Lakes Mall and pulled into Lavern White's driveway, a few minutes later. I turned my head and glanced at the three cars that slowly rolled by. One of them was a black Pontiac. The other was a green BMW, and the third, a white cab. Why the hell was there a white cab following me?

I was being trailed by a group of individuals, working together as a team—at least I hoped they all worked together. The chance of escaping one team was greater than the chance of escaping more than one. This shit was really serious.

I remained in my car for another minute, and to convince myself that what I was about to do, was best for my family and I. Family. I, Lexi, now had my own family to fighting for. Hard to believe, considering my past. I had a son, a husband and a mother with whom I'd re-established a beautiful friendship.

I was glad that my mother was here in the US with me. Moving her here was one of my best decisions, ever. She was excited to be here as well. She was also thrilled to know that there were many Jamaicans in Florida, which made her feel at home, thus helping to cushion the culture shock. She even introduced me to a Caribbean TV channel she'd become particularly fond of and had called me two weeks ago to let me know she'd settled into her Maryland home, and was able to access her favorite Caribbean channel there. She was happy to be able to keep up with Caribbean events and trends, while transitioning into the American culture. I was happy for her.

It was hard to imagine that, just as soon as things started falling into place, all hell started to break loose. My situation was hard to fathom.

"Mommy, are you ok?" my son asked, interrupting my thoughts.

"Yes, Lex. Your mommy will be just fine," I replied, suddenly exiting the car.

I hurried to the back passenger seat to let my son out of the car, retrieved my pocket book and son's overnight bag, and headed towards Lavern White's door. I pressed the buzzer, and waited.

Lavern and I were once friends, but hadn't been in touch since two years ago, when she claimed that my three year old son was bullying her five year old daughter. She made a big deal of the situation, and referred to my family and I as 'You People', meaning black people. See, Lavern is Caucasian, and her little remark didn't sit well with JT and I, so we agreed to stay away and keep our son away from Lavern and her child.

"Lexi? What are you doing here?" Lavern asked, opening the door with a hint of surprise.

"May we come in?" I asked.

Lavern eyed my son. "As long as you keep that little bully away from my daughter."

I glanced at seven year old Melanie, who was standing behind her mother, and wondered if Lavern was being for real. Had she just disrespected my son and I again? *Hold your tongue, Lexi. Finish the task at hand.*

"Of course, I'll see to it that Lex is on his best behavior," I forced a smile.

"Alright, come in," she invited hesitantly.

"Come on, honey," I said to Lex as I led him inside, and closed the door behind me.

"So," Lavern began smugly, "Did you come here to finally apologize?"

"Matter-of-fact, Lavern, I came here today because I realize that I needed you."

"Oh, really," she said, with a look of triumph.

"Well, I'll consider whatever you have to say to me, as long as we make some ground rules right this minute. You already know that your son is a bully, and we can't have anyone abusing my daughter in any way, shape or form. So, even if we become friends again, your son and my daughter can never be friends. Ok? Lexi, are we clear on that?"

Hell, no.

Instead of responding the wrong way, I bent over and kissed my son on his cherry cheeks. "Honey, go sit on the sofa over there and play with your PSP. Ok?"

"Ok, mommy. Am I a bully?"

"No, honey, you're a good boy. Come on, take your game, and sit over there, and don't move unless I tell you to. Got it?"

"Got it," Lexington said, and headed towards the sofa.

"Go upstairs to your room, Melanie," Lavern ordered.

I watched as seven year old Melanie strolled off.

"Lexi, your son needs to know that he's a bully. That's no way to grow a child-"

"May I borrow your cell phone?" I said cutting her off.

"Here," she handed me the phone.

I quickly dialed. Mom answered on the third ring. "Hello?"

"Oh, mom, thank god," I whispered, relieved.

"Mom, are you ok?"

"Lexi? How are you? Yes I'm alright, whose phone number is this?"

"A friend's, mom. I can't stay long, but we're in trouble. Whatever you do, do not call the house. Neither you nor your husband. Do not call the police, and do not use your telephone. Period. Just stay put until I figure this out. Got it?"

"Oh, Lord, is it Vaughnn again, honey?"

"Mom, shhh. I've got to go now."

I returned the phone to a confused Lavern. I was relieved that my mom was ok, at least for now.

"Lexi, what was that about? And why did you cut me off when I was calling you out on your son, and-"

"Let's get down to the real reason why I'm here," I said, cutting her off.

"What do you mean?" she asked, suddenly confused.

"I think we should have a seat at the table for this one," I suggested. "I also need a place to rest my luggage."

At the table, Lavern listened to me with a look of horror on her face. I ignored her expressions and continued to explain my story to her. I told her about the man I stabbed at the bus stop several years ago, the men who had rescued me that night, my sodomy against my step-father, the man my husband had killed in Jamaica, the people I'd help put in jail, and my husband's friend who'd been killed.

"Do you want some water?" I asked Lavern who had her palm over her heart and mouth wide open in shock.

"Lexi- I- I really don't understand- any of this. W-why are you telling-" Lavern busted out into a coughing fit.

"Let me get you some water and—"

"No- arhem! No water. I'm fine."

"Are you sure?"

"Lexi?"

"Lavern."

"Why are you here?"

I felt my lips part into a very small smile. *Gotcha. You bitch. How dare you belittle my son? If you think that my son is a bully, and you're scared of him, wait until you hear the rest of what I have to say to you.*

"Lavern," I began again, "While we were friends, there was a lot you didn't know about me."

"Ya think?" Lavern gasped.

"Well, now that you have an idea of my past, I think you're ready to help me."

"Excuse me?"

"Yes, Lavern. When I told you I needed you, I meant it."

"Ok, that's enough. Please take your son and leave my house."

"Can't do that, Lavern."

"Well then, I'm calling the police," Lavern said, rising from her seat around the table.

"Do that and you're dead," I whispered through gritted teeth. I quickly glanced around to mentally certify the children hadn't heard us.

"Are you threatening me?" Lavern pounded a fist on the table.

"Just hold your frickin' horses, ok? The men trailing me are probably outside watching us as we speak. They will make sure you-"

"There are men outside of my house?"

"Just sit back down, so I can talk to you."

"About what? We have nothing left to discuss. Please leave."

"Lavern, you are now involved in this, whether you like it or not. You had better sit down and hear me out."

Lavern sat in obedience, mouth wide opened in astonishment. Shit. She'd probably have a heart attack by the time I was done with her.

I explained the phone calls and threats against my family's life. I also expressed the possibility of my home being under surveillance, and my phones being bugged. I explained that I my every movement was being monitored.

"We were given six days to live. After that, they would take my family and I."

"What! This is all too much."

"They threatened to kill everyone in my life—even the babysitter. Chances are, you are now on the six-day clock."

"You are such an asshole! Is that why you came to my house—to use my daughter and me?"

"It was a move I knew no-one expected—"

"So you just show up here to put my life in danger? I have a daughter, Lexi, how could you have done this?" she cried.

I ignored Lavern's tears and retrieved the phone from my cargo pants. It had been vibrating since my arrival at Lavern's. Caller unidentified. Seemed my stalkers were already going crazy. They probably suspected I was up to something. Throughout all of their tracking endeavors against me, they'd never seen me visit Lavern's.

I also wasn't sure what they'd do with this new movement of mine, so I answered the call.

"Who is this?"

"What did I warn you not to do?"

"You warned me not to tell anyone."

"So what are you doing at Lavern White's house?"

"Spending a little time. I only have six days, remember? Furthermore, I'm leaving my son here so I can have some alone time with my husband tonight."

"Yeah-yeah-yeah. Bullshit. Now, listen. Tell your little girlfriend, Lavern, that she's now on our shit list, you get that? Tell her to start counting down. Call the police, and you're dead long before the six days are up."

The caller hung up, and a second idea struck me. I could easily wait until day six, and then call the police. I mean, what did we have to lose? Something was up. They were playing a game. It became apparent to me, that they planned on making their move way before six days were up. But they wanted to taunt me for a reason.

Suddenly, it hit me. The bastards were waiting for me to call my mother or for her to call me. They needed the location of my mom. They'd been trailing me for a while now. They knew that she was living with me. Then all of a sudden, she disappeared three weeks ago when she moved to Maryland to live with Tyrese. It had been a spur of the moment idea, after he captured her on a surprise visit to Florida. One moment they were out having drinks; the next, my mother was on a plane to Maryland. For good.

Good. I now had a theory to work with. It seemed that while we were being trailed and our home bugged, our cell phones hadn't been tapped until after my last conversation with mother two weeks ago after she arrived in Maryland.

My mom's sudden disappearance must have caught them off guard. Furthermore, she hadn't left with any luggage.

Whoever ordered the hit against me required my mother be included in the package. The assassins must have been getting ready to make their move when mom suddenly left. Ain't that something? Seemed they were way behind schedule and needed to make a move immediately. They were probably giving me the rest of the day to call mom, so they could scoop her up wherever she was.

This seemed to be a well-organized plan for revenge against me, which must have come at a very high cost. I wondered what price Vaughnn had been willing to pay to execute such a plot. Was I really worth all of that? My cell phone vibrated in my palm. I eyed the screen expecting another blocked call, but it wasn't. The number was unfamiliar, but the area code was not. 1-876. Someone was calling me from Jamaica. It had to be Uncle Desmond. I sent him to voicemail.

"Lexi, did you hear me?"

"Huh?" I said, returning from my thoughts.

"What you've done to me and my child is fucked up."

I didn't answer.

"How evil can one person be?" Lavern continued.

"Listen," I said cutting her off, "blaming me will not help you now. Like I said, you're already involved, so you might as well work together with me on this."

"Lexi, what the fuck!" she screamed.

"No cursing in front of my son, Lavern!" I yelled.

She flashed me a bitter glance. Bitch.

"You know what, Lavern? Forget that I came here. I'll just take my son and leave," I said, getting up to leave.

"What? You mean you wanna leave me by myself to face god-knows-who?"

"Then what do you suggest?"

"You shouldn't have come here in the first place."

"But I did. So what's it gonna be?"

Lavern shrugged, so I sat back down. I'd won.

"They're not after you- well, not really. I'm the target. My family and I mean a lot more to them, than you—"

"But they'll try to use me to get to you—"

"Not if I get to them first," I said, cutting her off.

CHAPTER TWENTY TWO
LEXI

"How do you plan on getting us out of this shit—if that's even possible?" Lavern asked me.

"That's a good question. I know that we're dealing with hardened criminals here," I replied. "We'll all go to the Pembroke Lakes Mall."

"So that's your big plan? To go to the mall?"

"No. Here's my credit card. Jump on your computer and book a flight to Maryland."

"A flight for whom?"

"A flight for my son, a flight for you, and one for Melanie."

"What? Why?"

"You're taking the kids to Maryland, to hide out at my mother's for the time being. Here's the address," I said retrieving my diary from my pocket book, and ripping a page from it.

My cell phone began to ring again. Unidentified caller. I ignored the call.

"Hurry. Boot up your computer and book a flight for tonight."

"Tonight?"

"Yes. Lavern; please hurry."

I watched as Lavern got to work; her hands and feet trembled like a leaf. I didn't have time to feel guilty about dragging her into this mess.

My cell phone continued to blow up. My heart pounded inside me.

I used my cell phone to call 411, and obtained the phone number to Jan-Ash Airlines. I used a second credit card to book a non-refundable flight for two to JFK, New York. Departure time: 10:25 pm. I looked at my watch. It was 4:45 pm. I had a few hours to get things together.

"I booked the flight for 7pm," Lavern said.

"No problem," I said.

"So, don't you wanna know the cost?"

"Not now," I said, eyeing my cell. It had suddenly stopped blowing up. I smiled to myself. So far, so good.

My decision to book a flight to New York was ingenious. That should keep the wolf pack busy for the time being. So I was right. They were hoping that I'd lead them to my mom.

"So why did you book a flight via your telephone, if you believe that it's tapped?" Lavern whispered.

"We don't have a lot of time. Grab an overnight bag for your kid and let's go!"

"Ok, here's your credit card back—"

"No, keep it. Once you get to Maryland, use it to purchase whatever you need. My mother will take care of my son."

"Oh. But why didn't we just call the cops?"

"Really, Lavern? And risk my son's life? The cops won't move fast enough. We'd all be dead by the time they showed up and gathered their information. Furthermore, we have no physical proof that we're being threatened. Do you get my drift yet?"

"I guess," Lavern replied.

"Once we lose them, we'll gain enough leverage to take them out—ven if it meant notifying the authorities. While you're upstairs gathering your things, call a cab to pick you up outside of the food court of the mall."

"Alright then," Lavern said, scurrying off upstairs. She caressed Melanie's face as they passed each other on the stairs.

I glanced over at my son who was still sitting quietly in the sofa, looking at me.

"Hey there, big guy," I smiled and walked over to him. My son was extremely smart. He knew that something was wrong. Bad men had threatened him, and Lavern had insulted him.

"What's up, buddy? Talk to mommy. Are you hungry?"

He shook his head.

"Are you sad?"

He nodded.

"Do you wanna go outside and play with me?"

"Yayyy!" he squealed.

"Melanie, do you wanna join us?"

"Yes!" she shouted.

"Lavern, I'm taking the kids outside to play!" I shouted.

"No!" Lavern shouted.

I ignored her stupid butt, "alright kids, outside we go!"

"Yayyy!" They both screamed in unison.

"The tickle-tickle monster is coming to get you!" I shouted as I chased them around in the yard. I knew I was being watched, so I braced myself and played my role. So far, so good.

Moments later when Lavern locked the door behind her and joined us outside, I wondered how she'd packed the overnight bag for Melanie, and made it back down those stairs so fast.

"Here comes a second tickle-tickle monster," she said with the fakest smile I'd ever seen.

"Do you guys want ice cream?" I asked.

"Ice-cream! Ice-cream!"

"Ok, everybody jump on the ice cream train!" I said, opening my car doors.

As I backed out of Lavern's driveway, my cell phone began to ring. My heartbeat intensified. This wasn't a good sign. They shouldn't be calling me right now. I thought that my plan had been working so far.

I placed the car in park, and examined my cell phone. I exhaled with relief when I saw JT's name dancing across the screen. I sent his call to voicemail, and started fired up my Bimmer once more.

Even though the kids were chattering away, and Lavern was sitting in the passenger right next to me, I'd never felt more alone. I only hoped that my plan would work. It was go hard, or die hard.

CHAPTER TWENTY THREE
LEXI

It was 5:50 pm when we arrived at the mall. I had paid attention to the behavior of the traffic and noticed that this time, I was only being followed by a green BMW. There'd been no black Pontiac in sight. I wasn't a professional, but I could tell that this was another good sign.

I sighed as I ran my sweaty palms over my cargo shorts. The blood from my injured knees had found its way on my clothes. I longed for a shower and change of clothing. I longed for my life to return to normal. I wished I hadn't tumbled over that gas pail and injured myself. This just had to be the longest, most horrific day ever.

Immediately after entering the mall, I stopped a young lady to praise her outfit and shoes. She was most delighted, and began to babble away about the shoe stores she's frequented, the prices for various shoes, and so on. Women could be so ridiculous. But this had worked to my advantage, since my goal was to create a diversion.

I turned around to a confused Lavern and encouraged her to take the kids for ice-cream without me. She finally caught up with my drift, and headed towards the food court, with the kids. I was a bit surprised that Lavern could be this slow, and prayed that she had called the cab like I'd told her to. If Lavern hadn't called the cab, then it was all over for us. This worried me, because she'd rushed up and down those stairs really fast, earlier when we were at her home. Maybe I'd made a mistake by getting her involved.

I didn't even get a chance to kiss my son goodbye. Couldn't risk things looking too suspicious. My heart ached as I resumed my conversation with the naïve woman, in the red and white outfit, that made her look like an oversized mint ball.

At 7:10 pm, I pulled out of the parking lot, shocked that I'd successfully managed to save my son. I knew this, because Lavern sent me a text message three minutes ago.

"We're on our way!"

I was elated. So far, so good.

As I was driving home, out of nowhere, an Escalade suddenly appeared at a stop sign on the east end of 172nd Street; swerved onto the main street and stopped in front of me, blocking my BMW.

Wendy suddenly jumped out of the vehicle and raced towards me. My heartbeat accelerated as adrenaline kicked in. I quickly retrieved the gun from my pocket book and rolled my window down. I had no more time or energy left for her bullshit.

I rolled my window down, finger on the trigger, I aimed the gun at her and greeted the bitch with a smile.

"Hello, stranger!"

"Hold, hold, hold!" she promptly raised both hands in the air as a sign of surrender to me.

"I'm in a hurry, so get your damn vehicle out of my way, or I swear I'll do it myself—and it's not gonna be pretty!"

"I don't want any trouble—"

"Too late! Move it!"

"I just wanna tell you that your husband is not who you think he is—"

"I'm guessing you know exactly who he is."

"You don't have to be sarcastic 'n shit. Listen, can you put that away so we can talk? Woman to woman— let's just talk. Ok? Let's just—"

"Shut up! Just shut the hell up, and let me pass. Last warning!"

"Ok. Ok. I'm leaving. But before I go, before I move my car and let you return home to that- that-godforsaken husband of yours, I'm gonna let you know that he don't love you. Hell, he don't even like you. He be sayin' some slick shit concerning you..."

A driver pulled up behind me and started honking his car horn. Wendy took off, got into her vehicle and sped away.

I put the gun away, exhaled, and went on my way.

CHAPTER TWENTY FOUR
LEXI

I drove home in deep thought. What did all of this mean? What was going on with JT?

I thought about his response to me earlier when I confronted him about Wendy's accusations. *"Jesus! Lexi, don't you know me by now? I would never discuss you or our relationship with anyone at all— let alone the women I sleep with."*

No. Wendy was nothing but a lying whore. JT would never get down like that. He'd never do me like that. Ever.

The ringing of my cell phone startled me. The caller ID announced that my husband was calling again.

"Hi, Babe," I was shocked at my own greeting. However, whether I wanted to be cordial with JT or not, I needed to stick to my plan.

When I was alone with him again, I'd further air my concerns.

"What's going on, Lexi? Where have you been? Where is my son? I've been so worried—"

"I know, I know. But I'm fine. We have a NY flight scheduled for 9 pm tonight."

"You have a what- for when?" he asked.

"I'll tell you about it when I arrive."

"Let me talk to my son."

"He's at the mall with Lavern and Melanie."

"He's at the mall with whom?"

"Honey, I'm feeling exhausted. Can we talk about this when I get home? I'm less than a few minutes away."

JT disconnected the call. I could tell that he was pissed. I placed the phone on the passenger seat and thought about the letter inside my bag. I decided that I'd just read it while JT and I were on our way to the airport.

CHAPTER TWENTY FIVE
LEXI

When I arrived home, I noticed that JT had secured the broken window with lumber. I chased upstairs to quickly pack the important things that JT and I would need for our travel. I took a few minutes to quickly shower and change the bandages on my knees.

"Where is Lexington?" JT asked, as he entered the bathroom. He scared me a little. I'd never seen JT this way before— there was something eerie about him.

"You look like hell," I replied nonchalantly, stepping past him into the bedroom.

"Lexi, where is my son? I'm not gonna ask you again."

"Let me get dressed first, and then I'll tell you all about it," I said, quickly slipping into my panties and bra.

"I need you to start talking now," he ordered, glancing at my breasts. I thought of all the times he made love to me, yet, today in the garage when I'd injured myself, he turned away from me.

"JT, stop acting like this. I told you that our son is with Lavern," I said, throwing on my blue Apple Bottoms and black hoodie.

"Don't play this game with me, Lexi. I need to know what you did with my son!"

"Don't yell at me."

"Lexi—"

"Alright!" I said, slipping my feet into a pair of black Nikes. "JT, let's go for a walk outside—get some fresh air. Ok?"

I was relieved that he'd finally listened and accompanied me down the stairs.

JT and I stepped out into the night air.

"Lexi, what happened to my son?"

"He's fine. Just hear me out; I figured out what's going on. I figured out a way I can save us," I whispered.

"What do you mean? Why did we have to come outside to talk, when you know those fools are watching us?" JT asked sarcastically.

"JT, our phones have been tapped; we're under surveillance. It's possible that they could hear everything we say inside that house. They're waiting for my mother to come back before they take us out, JT. I even think they plan on making their move tonight."

"They gave us six days—"

"It's a trick, JT. The situation is worse than we could ever imagine."

"So what did you do with my son?"

"I sent him to Maryland to stay with my mother—"

"What the fuck?"

"It's the best decision for him right now. The assassins don't know my mom is in Maryland—"

"Did they tell you that?"

"Who?"

"The assassins. Did they tell you they don't know your mom is in Maryland?"

"C'mon JT, work with me here. I figured all of this out on my own..."

He suddenly folded his fists, turned his back towards me and groaned angrily. He stormed off towards the house, but quickly walked back to me.

"Who's taking care of my son while he's out of our sight, Lexi? Who could you have entrusted our son to?"

"Lavern," I replied, wondering what the hell was JT's problem.

"You mean you turned our son over into the hands of a woman who hates black people, and hates our son even more?"

"JT, stop it," I scowled. Don't be unfair. Our family is in danger and I'm trying to help—"

"What's this I hear about us going to New York?"

"Oh, I booked our tickets for New York and—"

"These people that are stalking us; they're watching us like hawks, and you think they'll allow us go anywhere?"

"But, that's it, JT, I figured out—"

"Lexi, I think you should travel alone tonight."

"What?" I asked, stunned. "JT, you haven't even allowed me to explain.

"Go to New York by yourself. Ok?"

"JT, hold up; let me finish—"

"Lexi, it's over. We're done. There is no more you and me. We are finished!"

"What?" I gasped, shocked as hell.

"You've made your decisions on your own. They are your decisions. You should abide by them. I'm going inside to figure a way out for myself."

"You can't be serious."

JT turned and walked away from me.

"JT!"

But he didn't turn back.

Was all of this really happening to me in one day? I headed inside and went upstairs to collect the things I'd packed. I needed to get to the airport.

As I exited our townhome, I spotted JT heading up the stairs. I considered my pocket pistol, but continued on my way. Now was not the time to react to JT's bull.

CHAPTER TWENTY SIX
JT

I realize that what I did may seem grimy as hell, but Lexi is full of shit. At a time when my family needed me the most; needed me to be THE man of the household, Lexi, my wife, stepped up in my stead, and solely made the decision to turn my son over into the hands of a stranger; a stranger who hates my son; a stranger who was at war with my family. For all I knew, Lavern could be the one who was setting us up to get killed.

Lexi hadn't even contacted me after making the decision; as a matter-of-fact, I'd been calling her all day, and she'd ignored my calls. Every decision she made today was without my knowledge or consent.

I have never argued with Lexi. I'd spent years holding my tongue out of respect for all she's done for me. But now I realized that it was time to cut her loose.

I'd grown tired of Lexi running around town, acting as if she was the boss of me. Lexi continued to behave as if she was the man of the house, as if I was a little punk, and— I ain't no punk!

She made her plans on her own, so let her execute them on her own. Damn it man. My son was gone, without me getting the chance to say goodbye, and I know that my little man misses me, wherever he was right now. Where was he right now? The thought of him possibly being in harm's way, made my stomach knot.

I dimmed the lights in the house and went upstairs to lie down. While I was upstairs, I considered setting the alarm, but was too tired to go back down. Furthermore, fuck the alarm. What did it matter anyway? There was no way out of this shit, and my son was gone. I broke up with my wife last minute, and she was now on her way to getting killed.

Whatever happens to her now, I'm just glad I made sure that I broke up with her while I still had a chance. I'm glad I got my revenge against her. I hadn't realized until tonight, just how much I really hated Lexi.

Sleep was beginning to kick in. The load was too heavy for me to bear. My son was gone.

Life can be a real bitch at times. I mean, I left Jamaica years ago, running away from gunmen who were after my life. I now found myself in the same damned predicament. My involvement with Lexi had only delayed the inevitable. Any moment now, some fool could just pounce up on me and take my life— just like that. There is no way out of this shit.

You know what? All of this is Lexi's fault. If she hadn't been a snitch; if she'd held out and not cooperated with the FBI five years ago, we probably wouldn't have to be looking over our shoulders right now. I can honestly say that Lexi is the cause of all of this mess. In her quest to be 'Miss Big Bad Lexi', she'd ended up ruining all of our lives.

My thoughts wandered to my car that was parked in the garage downstairs. Maybe I could get the hell out of here without being spotted, but where the hell would I go? I threw a crystal vase across the bedroom floor....

CHAPTER TWENTY SEVEN
LEXI

I hauled myself and an overnight bag into the white cab that awaited me outside of my yard. Good thing I'd called a cab instead of driving my weary soul to the airport. I glanced at my cell phone. I hadn't heard from my attackers since I booked my flight to New York. The time was 7:55 pm. I had to assume that my plan had been successful so far. I was sure my attackers believed that I would lead them to my mother. But they didn't know I knew that.

Too bad that JT hadn't given me a chance to explain. Too bad that JT had left me. JT had left me. My family was no more. JT, once again, had acted up, just as he'd done years ago, and caused us our protection.

"Miami Airport," I said to the cab driver who eyed piercingly through his rearview mirror.

The cab pulled off, and I was soaked with painful thoughts once again.

JT hadn't said it, but he behaved as if I had been the cause of what's happening to us. I couldn't understand it. Not only had he lied, and cheated on me, he had chased me out of his life as if I was less than a person. I, Lexi, who had done so much for JT, given up so much to save his ass, had now been dismissed from his life like a used rag.

It devastated me when I considered how I married JT five years ago, just so he could acquire his legal stay in the US, to prevent him from having to return to Jamaica, where gunmen laid in wait for him. I recalled how I'd given up the love of my life, in order to marry JT—a decision which could possibly be the primary cause of our predicament. And now, when gunmen were after us, JT had completely abandoned me.

I couldn't bear to think about JT's betrayal, so I switched my thoughts to the vehicles I spotted trailing me earlier. The green BMW. The black Pontiac. The white cab. Earlier, on my ride back home from the mall, I'd noticed that neither of the three vehicles, including the white cab, was following me. It was good to know that I had given them something to keep them busy, but it wasn't good to know that they were following me in the first place. And why the hell was I being trailed by a white, New Horizon's cab? Who was in it? Where the hell was it?

Oh, my god! I had instructed Lavern to call a cab, but I recalled having my doubts about whether or not she did. She had gone up those stairs and returned pretty fast. How could she have secured her daughter's things, called a cab, and joined us outside so quickly? Did she not remember to call the cab, and ended up jumping into the suspicious cab with my son and her daughter? Or had she called a cab, and the cab driver, who had been following me, accepted Lavern's offer, picked her up with the kids, and took off with them?

Or, was JT right? Could Lavern really be trusted—especially with my child? I for one knew that karma was a bitch. Would Lavern sell me out to my pursuers in order to save her ass, just as I'd done to Vaughnn so many years ago?

Was it possible that my son, Lexington, was dead?

I grabbed my left breast as I regurgitated a little. Had I single-handedly ruined everything? Was my life now over?

Too many thoughts. Too many questions. My fear of the unknown overwhelmed me. For the first time in my life, I felt like giving up. Why hadn't Lavern contacted me again? No. No more questions. I'd already been through too much for one day.

I stared at my cell phone again. I wanted to take a chance and call Lavern to see if my son was alright. But my paranoia prevented me from contacting anyone. No telling who was tracing my calls. No telling just how far this phone-tapping thing could go.

I didn't smoke, but I desperately needed a cigarette.

"Do you have a cigarette?" I asked the cab driver. My body was shivering like a leaf in the wind.

"No," the cab driver replied.

Cab driver. I looked up in horror at the rearview mirror, and our eyes made four.

"Are you ok?" he asked, staring at me.

"Why do you keep staring at me like that? What is it?" I asked, horrified.

He removed his gaze from the rearview mirror without speaking.

My heart continued to race. Well, there had been only one cab trailing me. I hoped that this was the one, for the sake of my son.

Numbed with pain and fear, I looked out through the windows at my surrounding. So far, the driver of the cab hadn't detoured or done anything like that. There was nothing strange about my cab ride so far, besides the fact that the driver kept looking at me weird. I pulled my pocket book closer to me, and thought about the handgun inside it.

I'd become an emotional wreck within less than a 24 hour period.

I decided against asking the cabby for a cigarette. Or, had I already asked him for one? I was confused, and could no longer think straight. I needed something that would get my mind off of things, even a little bit.

My mind wandered back to JT again. If it hadn't been for him, my life would have possibly turned out differently. Possibly. But I'd made a promise to myself years ago, to never regret the good I do for others. Regardless, that didn't ease the pain. I didn't regret having assisted JT, but I felt as if I'd been used. I'd given up so much, and continued to hurt from sacrifices I'd made for the ones that I loved. It hurt to know that no-one cared enough to even acknowledge that. It really hurt.

Look at the shit I've been going through, since I was a child, till now. It seemed as if it will never end until I am dead—which could be much sooner than later. Look at all the things that I've been through, and how hard I've had to fight to survive? Yet, so many people have so many things to say about me. Lexi is crazy. Lexi is an evil bitch. Lexi is this, Lexi is that—well fuck you! Lexi is Lexi, dammit.

I couldn't escape the thoughts in my head. I needed a distraction—and quickly—before I exploded. The envelope. Yes. I shifted things around, rummaging through my belongings in an attempt to find the envelope I had retrieved from the mailbox earlier— the one that was addressed to me, with no return address. I couldn't find it. Where was it? I paused for a brief moment, inhaled, and thought for a second. My pocket book. The envelope is in my pocket book. I opened up my pocket book, retrieved the envelope, and opened it up. I wish I had known better than to open up the envelope. But I didn't. And so, my nightmare worsened.

CHAPTER TWENTY EIGHT
LEXI

Enclosed within the envelope was a folded handwritten note. Wrapped inside the note, was a typed letter. Puzzled, I decided to read the handwritten note first.

Lexi,
I wrote the enclosed letter with great regret and hesitance. I've been travelling around with it for days now, wondering whether I should submit it to you or not. However, today after your husband's discourteous display towards me, and your mention of my life possibly being at risk, I'm placing this envelope with enclosures into your mailbox.

Brimming with curiosity, I quickly unfolded the referenced letter, and continued to read.

Dear Lexi,
Your husband JT is a womanizer, and a heartless one at that. We'd met each
other and fell in love approximately six years ago, right before you and your family were enlisted into the Witness Protection Program. At the time, I was his nurse. I'm sure you can recall the shooting incident which landed him in the ICU.

Please be aware that JT had been very upset at your decision to "rat out" your ex-boyfriend, Vaughnn, and could never understand why you would put the lives of your family at risk, by testifying in court against Vaughnn. JT regularly verbalized his disgust for you and wished he didn't have to leave his entire life behind, in order to assume a new identity, and further spend the rest of his life pretending to love—according to him—"a self-centered bitch" such as yourself.

You may not know this, however, after you all disappeared, JT had contacted me and expressed how miserable and stuck he felt, being tied to you. He complained of your constant efforts to emasculate him. He had plans of ditching the protection program, and his life with you and Lexington, to return to Pembroke Pines and start a life with me. Well, at least that's what he had told me. During his rant, he also stated, "I curse the day I married that evil bitch for my green card." After it was discovered that he'd broken the rules and compromised your identity and safety by contacting me, the US Marshals intervened and relocated you all to Cincinnati. I believe you were all given new identities all over again.

I know all of this because JT later contacted me again, to update me on what had happened. He also advised me of all the people to whom he'd disclosed his true identity. His continued disrespect towards you and the system that protected him, was his plan of getting kicked out of the program so he could be with me again. This has ultimately led to your demise. I say demise, because you were all thrown out of the program, and I'm sure you have been trying to decipher JT's actions, even to this day. Haven't you been wondering why JT was so fixed on returning to Pembroke Pines to live—even if it meant risking your lives? Well, I was the cause of that decision. JT placed your lives at risk, in order to get more of me. He never could get enough of me. He was ecstatic when you agreed to return to South Florida and live in Weston, as it was close enough to Pembroke Pines, where I lived.

Anyway, about two weeks ago, I went through his cell phone while he was in the shower. I found numerous text messages of him corresponding with a woman who currently resides in Jamaica. I believe her name is Tanisha. What I'd unearthed that day devastated me, because JT had planned on divorcing you and running away with me as soon as he received his green card.

Instead, he'd been texting Tanisha, telling her how much he couldn't wait to finally be free of his wife, so he could make her his new wife.

As hurt and astonished as I was, I decided not to confront JT. Instead, I immediately hooked back up with my ex-boyfriend. A few days later, JT caught us kissing. The bottom line is that, I hurt JT before he could hurt me.

I'm sorry to have used my position as 'babysitter' to be closer to your husband and adorable son, but this was all JT's idea.

JT had been able to play you all these years because he knows you so well, he's even said it himself ever so often and ever so boastfully. Though I'm devastated that he ended up playing me—which 'they' all eventually end up doing—I comforted myself in knowing that he played you the most; being his wife, baby's mother, and all.

Do whatever you may with this information. By the time you read this, I'll be long gone. I always knew that your past would come back to haunt you;

which is why I've organized my way out of South Florida, and out of your miserable lives.

Please kiss Lexington for me.

Yours truly,
Carlecia-

"Cabby! Spin this shit around, now!" I yelled at the cab driver.

The tires screeched against the road as the cab driver hurriedly veered into the immediate exit ramp. I drew my pocket book closer to me and quickly thought of ways in which to make JT pay. I wouldn't shoot him. I needed him to suffer. I needed him to suffer greatly, and then die.

I figured out the perfect means of putting his lights out, and I planned on utilizing such means to execute my revenge against the son-of-a-bitch who literally ruined my fucking life.

"Can't you drive any faster?" I barked at the cabby.

He floored the gas pedal of the taxi and within minutes we were sailing north on I-95.

I looked up at the rearview mirror once again. Once again, my eyes made four with the cab driver's. I could easily send a bullet through the back of his head. Blow his brains out. Why did he keep looking at me so strangely? Was he the one who'd been stalking me? If so, why hadn't he made his move as yet?

"Don't fucking look at me like that!" I screamed, clutching the sides of my head with each palm.

I observed as he shuffled awkwardly in his seat. Any sudden move and I'd bust a cap in his head. He better not fuck with me right now. In fact, everybody should stay the hell away from me right now.

I checked my watch. It was 8:10 pm. I needed to arrive at the Miami Airport by 9:45 pm latest. Shit! Time was against me. But I needed to make this particular move.

With thoughts of JT's deadly betrayal, which had possibly led to the death of my precious son, I had absolutely nothing to lose at this point.

"Faster!" I shouted, "we need to return to Weston ASAP."

CHAPTER TWENTY NINE
LEXI

Instead of taking the regular route home, I directed the cab driver to make a left on 166th, and travel through the back streets of Weston until we were about one block away from where I lived.

"Wait here for me," I told the cab driver, who dared not look at me anymore. I exited the cab, sensing his confusion. His confusion confused me. Who was he? If he tried to attack me by the time I slipped into the dark bushes, I wouldn't be surprised at all. If he didn't attack, but disappeared by the time I returned, I also wouldn't be surprised at that either. Hell, nothing could surprise me at this point.

I checked my cell phone. Still no activity. The time was 8:25 pm.

I walked briskly through the bushes, and mentally dared him to leave with my luggage. I mean- I had the most important things with me in my pocket book, but I still dared that retard to drive away with my belongings.

Six and a half minutes later I was standing in the shadows of my backyard, at 8:31 pm.

I slipped my hands into my gloves and listened closely to the sounds of the night. I could hear the sounds of lizards, frogs and crickets. But there was something else: the sound of leaves breaking in the bushes. I wasn't alone. I whipped my head around. The sound halted. I was being followed. Someone was behind me, but who?

I turned around, reached inside my pocket book, and clutched my handgun. Before I could take out the gun, someone pounced on me from behind. A heavy blow from his elbow sent me and my pocket book lunging forward. I hit the ground hard. I tried to scream but was incapable of sound. Pain and darkness blocked my vision as I rolled over and looked up at the dark silhouette that was now hovered over me.

I glanced to the side and noticed my pocket book lying several feet away. A few feet away from my pocket book, was a luggage that resembled a brief-case. It must have belonged to my attacker. I wondered what was in it. I quickly returned my focus to the dark shadow, just in time to dodge a deadly blow from his fist. His knuckles cracked as they collided with the ground. He wailed. Before he could recover, I quickly locked his foot into my legs and twisted. He plummeted to the ground on his side. I sent a firm blow to his jewels. He wailed and writhed, grabbing his crotch. I was positive he hadn't expected this type of reaction from me. He probably thought that I was weak. I had absolutely no karate skills whatsoever. My moves had been inspired by thoughts of my son.

I flipped up to my feet, and kicked my assailant—twice in the crotch, and three times in the face. I could bet there was blood on my Nikes. My body pulsated with pain, but I ignored it. I couldn't afford for my attacker to recover. He'd kill me easily. With all my might, I kicked him again. This time in his side. I sent another blow to his crotch. While he continued to squirm about in agony, I fetched my silencer and capped him in his knee. He screamed so loudly, the lights switched on in the house across the street. I waited a while for the lights in my house to come on next. But they didn't. Good. I removed his mask. He was a white man. It hadn't been the cab driver at all.

"Who sent you?" I asked. No response, only cries of agony.

"Alright. Don't fucking answer," I said.

I ignored my own suffering and dragged my assailant through the back yard. Due to the darkness I couldn't see it, but I was positive there was blood everywhere.

"If you move or make a sound, I will shoot off your dick—no pun intended!" I warned, looking around wondering what to do with the bastard. He'd slowed me down big time. I hadn't plan for any of this. I checked the time on my watch. It was 8:38 pm.

I unlocked the kitchen door and immediately raced to disarm the alarm system. But there was no need to. It seemed as if JT had forgotten to arm the house before going to sleep. What a jackass.

I returned to the kitchen, grabbed a few of my kitchen towels, balled them up together, and stuffed them in my victim's mouth. I smiled at the thought of him being my victim. I'd actually fought him and won. I opened up a drawer and retrieved from it JT's duct-tape, which I used to bind the hands of my attacker. I dragged him into the garage, leaving trails of blood everywhere. I didn't care that my floors were all bloodied; moments from now, if I moved quickly enough, none of that would matter anyway. Even though I hoped with all my heart that all incriminating evidence would be destroyed after I was through executing my spur-of-the-moment plan.

"I have to go upstairs to check on my husband," I said, with one arm akimbo. "Now, how do I get you to stay put?" I asked, biting my lips in deep thought.

"Oh! I know," I said, reaching for my husband's tool box. I retrieved from it a hammer, and then two seconds later, found a big enough carpentry nail.

My victim shook his head violently, his eyes pleading for me not to do it.

"But I have to restrain you," I reasoned, looking down at his bloodied pant.

"Were you the one that called and threatened JT and I?" I asked. "Oops you can't answer with that thing in your mouth. Ok, just shake your head or nod."

He shook his head, eyes bulging in fear.

"So, you weren't sent here to make me suffer? Gimme your foot!" I said, referring to his uninjured foot.

He withheld his foot and continued to shake his head.

"You're a liar. You know?"

He continued to shake his head.

"Hmm- tell you what. I won't nail you to the floor. I'll just end up waking my husband—and we don't want that. Stay right here, and do not move," I said, placing the tool box out of reach of the trespasser. I lifted the gas pail, the one I'd tripped over a few hours prior. I ignored his pleading moans and poured gas to the floor as I exited the garage. I locked the garage door and gassed all of the first floor. I continued to pour gas as I walked up the stairs. Our bedroom door was slightly ajar, so I slid inside and saw that my husband was sound asleep. For now. Only a little bit of gas remaining, so I sprinkled some outside the bedroom door. I quickly crept into my son's room, to make sure he wasn't there. I needed to be positive he hadn't somehow returned while I was out. My heart broke all over again, when I saw that his room was empty. This was definitely my day to suffer.

All of this was JT's fault. I sprinkled the remaining gas outside my son's bedroom door, and cautiously sneaked back downstairs and back into the garage.

"Hold this," I ordered, and then watched as my victim awkwardly held the gas pail with his bounded hands.

"Wait a minute. Remove your damn gloves," I watched as he complied.

Good. I hadn't planned for any of this, but things seemed to be going straight. His fingerprints would now be on the gas pail.

"Carry it with you," I said, dragging him by his uninjured foot, towards the direction from which we had entered.

On my way out, I grabbed a lighter and a sheet of newspaper from a kitchen drawer. As soon as we were outside, I fired up the newspaper, threw it inside, and watched as a blazing fire quickly followed the gas trail, dancing vivaciously to the song of its freedom. I capped my bounded victim once in the head. I checked his pulse. He was dead. I removed the duct-tape from his hands. Then I removed the gag. I placed any incriminating evidence inside my pocket book. I checked the time. It was 8:52 pm.

I rushed through my backyard and disappeared into the night.

CHAPTER THIRTY
D'MONEY

"How many brothas fell victim to tha streetz
Rest in peace, young nigga, there's a Heaven for a
'G'
Be a lie, if I told ya that I never thought of death
My niggas, we tha last ones left
But life goes on..."

Life goes on. Words of the late Tupac Shakur echoed in my mind. My boys were all dead. They'd all been killed, while the reason for their death was still alive. But tonight was gonna change all of that.

I now had e'rythang I needed to bring her lots of pain. Tonight's the night I would finally swoop in and make my attack. I was prepared, and ready for this.

I checked the time in the cab. It was 8:05 pm. Shortly after this, I'd arrive at Lexi's house, ready to make my move.

It was Friday night. It's been almost one year since I'd been clockin' her moves —watchin' her family. Lexi and her family had the same routine on Fridays. But today, the routine had changed.

Her husband had come home early, and Lexi had left him at the house and taken her son to a house I've never seen her visited before.

While I was in the area, an offer came in to pick someone up outside the food court of the Pembroke Lakes Mall. The information said something about a woman waiting with two children. Cool,I was in the area already. Why not accept the offer? I checked the details again. The woman's name was Lavern.

Just as I was about to accept the offer, a text message came in on my cell phone. It was Shug-B letting me know that the chloroform was ready, and that I needed to come get it ASAP.

I recalled contemplating for a few minutes. Just as I was about to drive off, I spotted Lexi's car pulling out of the driveway. So I trailed her again, this time, to the mall. I wondered why she was so busy, and figured she must have been taking her kid to buy toys and shit. There was one thing I was confident about, and it's that Lexi would return home with her son. I had been clocking their movements for years now- well- five years ago she had fallen off of the grid. But she had resurfaced. I had first seen her about two years ago at that Caribbean restaurant her idiot husband owns. I had been clocking their moves since then, so I had no reason to doubt my instincts. Lexi would return home, for sure, with her son, and JT would leave out at his regular time.

Anyway, it seemed that Lexi was some sort of real estate agent, but as the months went by, she worked less and less. Maybe that was due to the slowed economy. She didn't even seem to mind, as her husband managed some type of lumber store, and owned that Jamaican restaurant I was tellin' you about. Ain't that sumthin'? These wet-backs left Jamaica and came to my country; stabbed me; had my homeboys killed; now worked at some fancy job; drive around in fancy cars—basically livin' the kind of life I've only dreamed of. I mean, I could easily live like that, but for how long? The popos would lock me up. Yet, here's this Jamaican heifer and her cocky ass husband, surviving successfully in America, while I, an American citizen born and bred, had to be scrounging around for crumbs.

It's just like I've always said. The American system is fucked up. How many times had I been jailed for trying to survive in America? Yet, here were these punk ass immigrants living like kings and queens in my country.

There was no more hate left inside me. I couldn't possibly hate Lexi, and all that she represented, any more than I already did. I truly despised her. Fo' real, fo' real.

First, I planned on takin' out her son. I'd make him suffer, and then kill him while they watched.

Second, I'd take out the cocky bastard, slow and steady, while she watched. And then I'd keep her captive and rape her every day for as long as she lived.

Yes. Tonight, tonight I'd be makin' my move. I've gone over this in my head several times.

Every Friday at 9:00 am, Lexi's husband leaves out to work. About an hour later, Lexi leaves out to get her hair and nails done. Then she goes grocery shopping afterward. She usually returns home between 2:00 pm and 3:00 pm, and maybe starts dinner before her family arrives back home. See, her babysitter, a voluptuous, Hispanic looking chic, usually takes Lexi's son on Thursday mornings. She usually returns with him the next day, Friday, at the same time the cocky bastard arrives home from work. He'd leave out again later at night at around 11:00 pm. I believe he was having an affair with the sitter, because I've trailed him to her house on several occasions. I was very pleased to know that Lexi's husband was cheating on her with the babysitter; thank you very much.

Anyway, I had it all planned out. Tonight, I'd pounce on JT while he's getting into his car, and take him out with this chloroform I'd gotten from my hook up. I'd drag him back to the front door and ring the doorbell. "Ma'am! Open the door; your husband just fainted!" Then I'd pull my gun on her as soon as she answered the door. With the gun to her head, I'd have her sit on the floor, faced away from me, and take her out with the chloroform.

Then everything would be smooth sailing after that.

I made a left on 166th and took the back streets into Lexi's neighborhood. I couldn't risk being spotted by anyone. In fact, I was already up to my ass in the number of disciplinary actions against me; one more strike, and I'd be out of New Horizon's, and out of a job. It didn't matter to me though. As long as things went according to plan tonight, New Horizon's Cab Services could kiss my ass. This is what I had spent the last eight years of my life living for.

I parked off to the side of the road, two blocks away from Lexi's house, stepped out of the cab, and fired up a blunt. I was giving myself sufficient time to get to Lexi's crib. I couldn't risk missing JT. I smoked my chronic and reminisced on my final night with my homeboys, eight years ago. I remembered how happy we were; rollin' around in my shiny, purple Cadillac with 22 dubs. Things had been going great for us, until I got stabbed by Lexi.

What had my boys done that night? They must have been the ones to call the police. Yeah. That's what must have happened. My boys called the police and left the scene, because they had a bitch tied up in the trunk of the car.

Whatever happened to that ho? How come the police hadn't questioned me about her? Sheeet- my homeboys musta gotten good rid of her that night before they were gunned down the next day.

Was it the weed? Or did I see a New Horizon's cab whiz right by me? I checked my watch. It was 9:01 pm. I highly doubt that I'd been spotted. From where I was parked it was impossible fo' anyone to notice me or my cab. Shit didn't make sense. Why was a New Horizon's cab sailing through the back streets at this hour of the night?

CHAPTER THIRTY ONE
UNIDENTIFIED CALLER

"Hello."

"Yeah- hey. It's me."

"What's the status? You have them all together yet?"

"Well- not quite- but almost."

"What the hell is almost?"

"They booked a flight to Kennedy Airport; I have reasons to believe that's where the mother is at."

"They left to New York and you let them get away? You know boss will be pissed. Instead of calling me, you should be planning your funeral."

"No, just hear me out. I'm in New York right now."

"Say what?"

"Yeah, In a few hours, Lexi and JT will be arriving at this very terminal from which I'm calling you."

"Where's Willow and Kappa?"

"I left them behind so they could keep an eye on the young woman with the kids. We identified her to be Lavern White from—"

"Hold the line. I think   Willow is calling me."

"Ok, I'll hold."

"Willow. Talk to me and make it quick."
"Yo, some crazy shit is going down over here."
"Haha, Willow, what are you talking about?"
"Yo, I don't even know where to start, mehn."
"Listen, I got Chin on the other line waiting to discuss something important. So just start from the beginning, and abbreviate your shit."
"Ok, Aight then. Uh- it was so much more efficient when there was three of us doing this together—"
"Willow!"
"Aight! We all heard that the chick had booked that flight to New York; Chin immediately booked his, so he could keep tabs on them. He believed that they would—"
"Lead him to Lexi's mother? I already know that part. Tell me something I don't know; Chin is waiting for me on the other line."
"Oh, so- Chin left us behind- me and Kappa, to keep our eyes on things. Everything appeared to be normal, until I ended up at the mall."
"Ended up at what mall?"
"Lexi took her son to Lavern White's house, and booked a flight for her and her husband there. Then

she, her son, Lavern and Lavern's daughter went to the Pembroke Lakes Mall."

"Why would Lexi go to Lavern's house to book a flight to New York? Did she use Lavern's computer?"

"No. She used her own cell phone."

"So she went to Lavern's house to book a flight to NY, using her cell phone, and you didn't find anything strange about that?"

"Ain't nothin' strange about that; she mentioned leaving the son at Lavern's so that she and her husband could spend quality time together before we zapped them."

"Quality time together? Yeah right."

"Why do you say that?"

"Just keep talkin, because you've all fucked up."

"How did you know- I mean- why did you just say that?"

"Just get to the point and be concise. I hardly have time to waste."

"Ok, where was I? Uh—"

"Willow, tell me something. While you allowed Lexi freedom to visit the mall, hadn't it occurred to you that you were being played?"

"Naw, it ain't like she knows that her phones have been   tapped."

"She knows, dammit!"

"I assure you, she doesn't."

"Oh, yeah? You better hope for your sake that you're right."

"Well, you can ask Chin. He organized the whole thing and—"

"Screw that. Tell me what happened after you followed them to the mall."

"Well, after we arrived at the mall, Kappa, decided to return to the station to keep an eye on JT."

"What the fuck are you saying to me, Willow? Why would both of you leave the station to follow Lexi?"

"That's what I'm saying. Everything got messed up. When I entered the mall, I noticed Lexi talking to a young woman, while Lavern took the children to the food court."

"So they split up."

"Yeah. Since I was the only one present that could keep tabs on Lexi, I kept my focus on her while I waited for Lavern to return with the kids."

"So what's the problem?"

"Lavern never returned with the kids."

"Wait, hold the fucking line, ok? Lemme tell Chin to hang up."

"Chin!"

"Yeah?"

"Seems like ya'll fucked up. Hang tight where you are until I call you back—I wanna hear this shit."

"What? Is it Willow on the other line?"

"I'll call you back."

"Hello, Willow; you still there?"

"Yeah, mehn, I'm still here. So basically, at the mall, the other woman- uh- Lavern, took her daughter and Lexi's son for ice-cream, while Lexi stayed behind to chat up a young woman wearing a red and white outfit. Lavern never returned with either child."

"Where are you now, Willow?"

"Outside of Lexi's house."

"Did Lexi return to her house?"

"That's it. Earlier, when Lexi arrived at her house, without her son, she and that fellow had a fight."

"What did they argue about?"

"I don't know. I couldn't hear what they were saying."

"Why? Did the equipment malfunction?"

"No. I- I couldn't hear what they said because they were outside."

"Haha. This only gets fucking better. So, Willow, at that point did it still not occur to you that Lexi might have suspected that her home had been bugged?"

No response.

"Willow, so now your ass has gone silent. How come you're just now notifying me about this shit? Tell me, where is Lexi and JT now?"

"Lexi left JT behind and went to the airport by herself."

"Hold on, so they split up again?"

"Y-yeah. I'm afraid so—"

"You're afraid so? Put Kappa on the phone!"

"I haven't seen Kappa."

"You're making me sin, with all this fuckin' swearin'! Willow, where the hell is Kappa?"

"I don't have a clue."

"So you gentlemen really fucked me over. Huh? You made an amateur, immigrant bitch outsmart you."

"I guess Lexi is smarter than we expected- it all happened so fast, none of us was expecting this. We'd given them six days to—"

"Six days? You mean you contacted them and threatened them? Without telling anyone? That wasn't the directives—"

"The directives came from Chin. He said he was paid to capture all four of them together, but the mother suddenly disappeared and you were on his ass—"

"So he went against my orders and screwed me over? What will I tell Vaughnn? What will I tell Politician Styles? Just tell me you're at least on Lexi's trail."

"That's the problem, boss- I mean- earlier I left Kappa at the station to keep an eye on Lexi's house. I left to check on Lavern White's house, s-so I could take Lexi's son. But there was no-one at the house, and when I returned to the station, Kappa was gone."

"So- where is Lexi?"

"I'm looking at her house right now, and the whole thing is ablaze."

"What do you mean by that? Did someone set it afire?"

"I don't know; I wasn't here at the time. There's nothing I could have done to prevent this. The entire neighborhood has come out to watch; it's like a horror show over here. I'll have to pack up and vacate the area before anyone notices me. Fire trucks, and police cars are everywhere, and Kappa is nowhere to be found. Hello? Did you hang up- hello? Hello!"

CHAPTER THIRTY TWO
D'MONEY

I checked the time again. It was 9:10 pm, nine minutes since the New Horizon's cab had whizzed by. I wondered if I was being watched. Had my boss been clocking my moves, the way I had been clocking Lexi's? Bullshit. It must have been the weed talkin'- straight up. I had no time to consider my boss, and gettin' caught and all that other bullshit.

I needed to remain focused, so I could properly execute my plan. Shit. Execute. Where the hell did I learn that word? Haha. It must be the weed that I had been smokin'. If I had gone to college, I'd prolly be a doctor today. As long as I got enough marijuana to smoke. I was smartest when high. Scientists need to start tellin' people the truth. Weed don't fry nobody's brain. Look at me!

I locked up the vehicle and quickly headed towards Lexi's house. The cool night air caressed my skin. My wild locks bounced up and down on my head, their movements matching my quick strides. For a prestige city such as Weston, there sure was a lot of bushes and darkness. Any second now a lion, or a tiger, or crocodiles and shit would attack me. I patted my jacket pocket. The packages were in place. Good. Shug-B- I'm sure you remember my dawg, Shug-B. Yeah, the one who got me outta the police chase. He promised that he'd show up at 11:30 tonight, to help a brotha out. He planned on driving his old pick-up truck. Yeah. My boy.

As I neared Lexi's home, I could smell smoke. I could tell the scent different from that of the weed I'd just whiffed up. I stopped in my tracks and observed smoke ahead of me. What the hell was going on? In the distance I could hear the excitement of firefighters yelling, sirens wailing, people conversing- conversating- whatever. I stood within the shadows and observed the chaos in Lexi's yard. Soot, smoke, fire and firefighters enveloped the area where Lexi's majestic house once stood. The fire seemed to have been ghastly. It was uncontrollable, and the firemen were working desperately through thick smoke to put out the last of it.

I sighed with deep despair and confusion. What the hell had happened—tonight of all nights? Where were Lexi and her family? Had they all been burnt to death? Dang! I should have known that shit wasn't right, the moment I noticed their routine had changed. I shouldn't have been so confident.

If Lexi and her family had burnt to death, then my prayers would have been answered, but I still wasn't one hundred percent satisfied. I wanted to take them out myself. Got-dang-it! I had waited years to personally take Lexi out, and this shit was happening tonight? What the hell!

Popos were everywhere; some were even coming out of the bushes on the other side with flashlights. I took a step back, and tripped over something that looked like some sort of briefcase. I wondered where the hell that briefcase had come from. I twisted my ankle. It hurt really badly, but I quickly managed to heave myself back up.

Why tonight? Fuck!

This was no time for me to wander about in the bushes, during an occasion such as this, at a scene such as this. I needed to bounce.

Disappointed, and bewildered, I took a few steps backward eyeing the scene one last time, turned around suddenly to bolt, and stumbled right into a police officer.

He coughed a couple times, could be from my stench, or the stench of smoke in the air.

"Officer Barkly, over here!" He yelled.

I was fucked.

"Turn around! Hands above your head!" he ordered.

My first thoughts were to take him out with the chloroform that was in my jacket pocket. Shit-chloroform! I was dead for sure. Suddenly I regretted foregoing the offer to pick up Lavern, for collecting the chloroform from Shug. Why hadn't I just accepted the offer? Dammit. There was still a bit of hope, however. If I could only manage to retrieve the chloroform from my pocket, I could take the officer out. I slowly reached for my pocket while I spoke.

"Listen, officer, I was in the area and noticed—"

"Hands in the air where I can see them!" he shouted.

I took a deep breath and raised my hands in the air. There was no way out of this now. How would I explain the gun? How would I explain the chloroform? Finally I'd be knicked for nothing. Life was indeed a bitch.

"Why are you wearing leather gloves?" he asked, pointing a flashlight at my arms.

"Officer, I- I always wear gloves."

"Is that right?" he asked suspiciously.

"Like I said officer, I was in the area, and noticed all the commotion- so I—"

"Read him his rights," Officer Barkly ordered as he approached.

Words couldn't express how astonished I was when the cops threw me to the ground, searched me, and found absolutely nothing.

"Alright buddy, you're taking a trip with us to the station."

My heart pounded within me, but I was also relieved. None of the stuff that was in my jacket pocket had been recovered by the cops. It seemed that they had fallen out when I tripped over that briefcase. Lucky me!

When I considered my situation, I was actually innocent.

They didn't know what my plans were. The only person who knew what I was up to, was Shug-B. And he wouldn't rat me out for nothin'. I really hadn't done anything wrong, so I really had nothin' to fear. Well- at least so I thought.

CHAPTER THIRTY THREE
UNIDENTIFIED CALLER

"Hello- finally you called back. It's been over three hours; what happened?"

"Tell me that Lexi is in your radar again. Tell me that she arrived at JFK, just like you suspected."

"I- I'm so sorry."

"What are you sorry about, Chin?"

"Sh-she never arrived."

"What are your thoughts on that?"

"I- I think that you were right. I think I truly screwed this one up—"

"Ya' think?"

"You have to admit that none of us expected any of this from Lexi—especially this quick after contacting her."

"So now you choose to inform me of your disregard for my orders."

"No- no- let me explain. I—"

"Where is Lexi?"

"I don't know."

"You're dead."

"Wait- hold on, I can explain this- don't hang up. Hello? Hello? Hello!"

CHAPTER THIRTY FOUR
LEXI

I wiped tears from my eyes and watched the clouds go by. The plane ride to Maryland had been a turbulent one, but I was glad to be in the air and safe. My comfy window seat was icing on the cake, the agent at the airport had really hooked me up.

Thoughts of my most recent deeds were blurred. All I could clearly envision was arriving at my destination safely, and having my son in my arms once more. I pushed all thoughts of everything else to the back of my head, and embraced hope. It was all I could do to keep myself going. I could no longer bear to wonder if my son was dead, and if Lavern had betrayed me. I dared not fathom her handing my mother's address over to the enemy. I couldn't stand to think that she would harm my son in any way, due to her hatred for him. I didn't want to decipher whether or not she hated black people.

The flight attendants were serving refreshments.

"Just a bottle of water for me, please- no ice," I said.

I readily collected my water and guzzled it all down in one go. Damn. I was glad there were no passengers next to me. The privacy felt good. I'd be better able to clear my head this way. It must have been destiny that had gotten me on this flight. Destiny had that pretty representative working the night shift, just so she could hook me up with a last minute flight to Maryland. Destiny even made it so the agent would offset the NY flight cancellation costs, with the cost of the new plane ticket.

I mentally dared Vaughnn's stale ass prison gang to assault me inside the airport. I wished that they would. But destiny would not have it so. It was destiny why I was still alive, even though I dared not contemplate the reason why. Was destiny to blame for all the crap I've endured? Was destiny playin' a fucking game with my life?

But, like I said, those thoughts, too, had to be pushed to the back burner of my mind, so I could effectively cling to hope. Destiny or not, Maryland, here comes Lexi.

CHAPTER THIRTY FIVE
LEXI

I had no luggage to collect at baggage claim. The only load I carried were two small bags, including my pocket book which had been cleared of all deadly weapons.

"Security!" I yelled.

A dark, average built guard stopped and turned around. I quickened my steps to the point of running so I could catch up with him.

"No need to run, gorgeous. Take your sweet time," he said smiling.

I was a bit disgusted. Men could be so idiotic at times. I hated when they smiled at me like that—looking at me all perverted and shit.

Moments later, I was standing face to face with the guard.

"My phone battery died. May I borrow yours?"

"You wanna borrow my phone battery?"

"No, your phone," I replied, flustered.

"I was only kidding. I knew you meant—"

"May I borrow it now, please? If not, I'll ask someone else; this is an emergency," I said cutting him off. He was being such a retard. A perverted, corny retard.

"Oh- uh- here you go," he said, handing me the phone, and acting as if his feelings had been hurt. Big baby.

My limbs weakened, and my heartbeat intensified as I waited for someone to answer my call.

"Hello?" she answered on the third ring.

"Mom!" I screamed.

"Lexi?"

"Mom!"

"Lexi, are you ok?"

"Yes, where's Lexing...." before I could finish my sentence, a kid in the background began to scream. *"Mommy!"*

"My son," I whispered, suddenly overwhelmed with emotion.

"Yes, we're all here. Lexi, where are you?"

"At the airport, mom," I said sniffing back tears.

"What airport, honey?"

"Essex."

"Ok, we're on our way. Tyrese, she's at Essex. Lexi, don't move a muscle. What flight—"

"Lentz Airlines; can I say hi to my—"

"Ma'am, I have to go," the security guard said.

"Mom, the guard wants his phone back, and I have to go. Kiss my son and tell Lavern I said—"

"Ma'am!"

"Don't ma'am me! Just a minute ago you were undressing me with your eyes. Here you go, pervert!" I disconnected the call and handed the guard his phone back.

"Remind me never to lend your ungrateful little ass my phone again!" he said, storming off in utter shock.

"That's no way to speak to me!" I yelled after him, "Where's your boss at?"

"Fuck you, fuck my boss and both of you can fuck me!" he yelled back.

Now it was my turn to be shocked. I cleared my eyes of tears, and looked around to see if anyone had noticed the brawl. People did notice, but nobody seemed to have cared, and the guard was now out of sight.

I found myself a good little corner where I could cry and wait patiently for my family to arrive.

CHAPTER THIRTY SIX
LEXI

I cozied up with a blanket on my mom's chaise, in front of the television. I awakened to the scent of brewed coffee, freshly baked biscuits, bacon, eggs and home-fries. I was starved. Food was the last thing on my mind, but my body had other plans. I hadn't eaten since breakfast the previous day. I'd made dinner for my family; however the sudden phone threats distracted us from eating. Mom's home smelled delicious.

I pressed the Guide button on the remote to find out the time; 9:33 am. This meant that my hot bath last night had successfully induced five hours of sleep. I navigated the TV guide in search of mother's favorite Caribbean channel.

As I searched, my mind wandered back to the horror of the previous day. And then it finally hit me. I had committed a double homicide before leaving Florida last night. Pangs of guilt and apprehension engulfed me. Anxiety suddenly crowded out the scrumptious smells of mom's kitchen. *Oh, god!* I murdered my husband.

"Lexi! You're up," mom announced as she entered the room with my son.

"Mommy! Mommy!" my son screamed, jumping into my lap.

"Hey there big guy," I said hugging and squeezing him.

"Mommy, where is daddy?" he asked after I released him from our embrace.

"He decided not to come along with me," I said. Technically, I wasn't lying. I fought back tears. How could I ever live with myself after murdering the father of my child? My son was now fatherless. If the police found evidence that lead to me, I'd go to prison for the rest of my life as well. The only good that could come out of that, would be the chance to kick Bonita's ass decently. I shook my head and dismissed those thoughts. I felt as if I was literally going crazy.

"Lexi, last night when we got in, you were beyond exhausted, so I didn't press you about JT. Tell me, what's the deal between you two," mom asked, taking a seat in her lazyboy.

Mom's new home was beyond cozy. If my life was normal, and I lived here, I'd be falling asleep every other minute. Such luxurious comfort had to be sinful.

"What do you mean, mom?"

"Well- you said that JT got upset with you, and sent you to Maryland by yourself."

"He didn't send me to Maryland- listen- JT got very angry when he found out that Lavern was on her way here with our son."

"So- you went behind his back?"

"I had to, mom!" I glanced at my son. His face was now sullen.

"Why are you sad, honey?" I asked, kissing him on his cherry cheeks, "Everything's gonna be ok, you hear me?"

"Ok," Lexington replied.

"Alright," I said placing him to stand, "mommy is exhausted. Go and play karate with Melanie." I watched him as he chased out of the room.

"You shouldn't allow your son to play karate with little girls."

"Mom, they're just kids."

"And you shouldn't be so chummy with him either. He's a boy."

"Are you saying I'm not supposed to show my child love?"

"I'm saying not to show him too much love."

"Mom, where's Lavern?"

"Still sleeping."

"Where's your husband?"

"Still sleeping."

"Oh," I said, wishing I could share my pain with her.

"Lexi, are you alright?"

"I will be," I said, struggling to hold back tears, while ignoring the void within me.

"How do we handle these threats, and the men behind the threats?"

"Let's figure it out later, when everyone's awake," I said, buying time. Truth is I no longer wanted to face any of this. I just wanted to spend this time in safety with my son. Thinking about the future was too frightful.

"As you wish," mom said getting up, "I'm going back to the kitchen where breakfast will be served in less than two minutes. Join me when you're ready."

"Hold on, mom, where's that channel you were telling me about?"

"Oh, hand me the remote, I'll find it."

I handed her the remote.

"I see I've sparked an interest?"

"I guess."

"You guess? It's high time you visited your birth-land."

"Yeah. I really miss Jamaica. The last time I was there was over six years ago- when I manhandled Everhard."

"I meant to ask you about that. He claims he has a vendetta against you, Lexi—"

"Yup. He abused me when I was a child, so I returned the favor."

"Lexi, did you—"

"I sure did."

"You didn't—"

"Oh yes I did."

"Lexi!"

"Wait- go back. That must be it," I said, referring to the Caribbean channel.

"Yes, it is. Here's the remote. Join me when you're ready."

"Ok, mom."

A music video lit up the screen as dancehall singer, Ladysaw, lyrically explains how she used her good pussy to acquire another woman's man.

We now interrupt our program to bring you this breaking news.

A man currently clings to life at the Mandeville Hospital, after being severely beaten, shot and left for dead, at a remote location deep in the woodlands of Manchester, Jamaica.

The victim, a 59 year old man, now identified as Desmond Jones, remains in critical condition.

Police officers responded to a 911 call, placed by rescuers, whose identities have not been released.

The callers told police that they recovered the limp, bloodied body of Desmond Jones during their commute to a local farm.

Desmond Jones later underwent surgery at the Mandeville Public Hospital where his condition was reported to CariVybz TV as being critical.

The ICU is currently being guarded by members of the police force.

The victim has alleged that Jeremy K. Styles, Ex-Prime Minister of Jamaica, ordered a hit against the life of Jones.

It was noted that approximately six years ago, Lexi Jones, niece of Desmond Jones, testified in a US court against Bonita Styles, Prime Minister Styles' daughter. Lexi's testimony led to the imprisonment of Bonita Styles, which induced the prime minister's rage against the Jones' family.

It is alleged that Minister Styles is out for revenge.

Further, police investigation has led to the recovery of several dead bodies, which are identified as Pollymae and Radclif Jones, Margaret Jones ..."

"Mom! Mom! Mom!" I screamed, jumping to my feet in horror. The remote control fell to the floor.

"Lexi, waapen, mon?" mom asked in Jamaican patois.

"Look!" I pointed towards the TV screen at the faces of Pollymae and Radclif Jones, my grandparents, who were recently murdered. My grief was insurmountable. This was more that I could bear. I turned around in sorrow to look at my mother.

"Turn that up!" mom shouted.

We couldn't find the remote. Where was the damn remote?

Tyrese and Lavern rushed inside the room, groggy eyed, and confused.

The news reporter continued.

"...stabbed multiple times. An interview conducted by our news team at a local jail, where Antonius Montique, nicknamed Everhard, gives us his version of the story.

"So, tell us, you are nicknamed Everhard, correct?"

"Yes! I am Selassie's son!"

"O-kay then, and you believe your detainment was in lieu of Politician Styles setting you up. Correct?"

"Yes, rasta! One day he was at I mon's house asking for Lexi's mother. The next minute I'm being locked up for murdering Lexi's grandparents—even though Politician Styles told me he had them."

"Them who?"

"Lexi's parents! He said he would get me a visa to America, if I gave him Sonia's whereabouts…"

I fell to my knees in agony.

"Wait a minute!" Tyrese said, "This is fucking serious."

"This is absolutely crazy!" Lavern said.

My mom remained dumbfounded.

Lexington and Melanie hopped into the room.

The news reporter continued.

"Everhard- or should I say, Mr. Montique, rumor has it that someone molested you some years ago. Is that accurate?"

"What the f%$@ does that have to do with anything? Fire pon yu blood—"

"Christine, back to you."

"Thank you, Angie. We'd like our viewers to be aware that the rest of the video cannot be aired at this time.

It was also alleged that other suspects involved are Dennis Marshall, Carlton Brown, and Sonny Moses Smith, otherwise known as Benji.

The three suspects absconded from the Parish of Manchester and are said to be in hiding.

If you have any information, please call the following toll free number at the bottom of your screen.

We now return to our scheduled program.

CHAPTER THIRTY SEVEN
LEXI

I could possibly be going to prison.

My grandparents, whom I loved more than life, were dead. Dead. My life as I knew it was now over. What was the purpose of all of this? Just so JT could acquire permanent stay in the US? Why wasn't he dead? How many lives could one man possibly have? How could he have possibly survived that fire?

I was back in Florida. Shortly after the devastating news that morning, mom's phones began to blow up. When I powered on my cell, immediately it rang. I felt my stomach churn as a police officer relayed the news to me.

"Mrs. Henry- your name is now Mrs. Henry, correct? Good. This is Officer Barkly. At first we believed that you were in the house with your husband at the time of the fire, but he managed to confirm with fire rescuers that you weren't-"

"What fire? What are you talking about?"

"Mrs. Henry, I am so sorry. Where are you? We would like for you to come down to the station—"

"Where is my husband? Did Vaughnn get to my husband?"
"A man was shot to death in your backyard..."

So, like I was saying, here I was, back in South Florida, and could possibly be going to prison. This is how it all went down.

We, my son and I, my mother and her husband, Lavern and her daughter, arrived a little over two weeks ago. We were staying at the Bella Villa Inn, located in Downtown Fort Lauderdale. .

Throughout this time we were being rigorously interrogated by the police. I was pretty sure that our stories were in sync. I maintained my story regardless of how the cops would come at me. I also believed I had a solid alibi, until yesterday when I was interviewed by Officer Lloyd. I was caught off guard.

"Mrs. Henry—"

"Call me Lexi."

"Ok. Lexi. I understand that this is a very difficult time for your family. I would like you to know that we are doing our best to have this case resolved and bring closure to you and your loved ones—especially Mr. Henry—your husband."

"I get it."

"I have a few routine questions I'd like to ask you, and then you're free to go. Is that ok?"

"Yes."

"Where were you on the night of October 16?"

"I already told you guys a million times. When my husband and I first received the threatening phone calls, we were horrified. I decided to take my child to Lavern's where I gave her my credit card so she could book three flights to Maryland, that same evening. After booking the flights, she used her cell phone to call a cab to pick her up outside the food court of the Pembroke Lakes Mall. As soon as we arrived at the mall, I created a diversion so that, she could disappear with my son and her daughter."

"Disappear?"

"Yes. We knew we were being followed, my phones were tapped, and my home was bugged. I figured the only way out was to split up so Lavern could safely get to the cab with the children."

"So the three flights booked were for—"

"Lavern, her daughter and my son."

"Was Lavern being threatened prior to your arrival at her home?"

"No- but—"

"So you endangered her life to save your son's."

"I took a risk."

"By endangering Ms. White and her child."

"I had no other choice."

"What is your relationship with Ms. White?"

"We're friends."

"Hmm. Why did you choose Lavern to be the scapegoat?"

"She was hardly a scapegoat. I chose her because of our history and because we haven't interacted for a long time. I knew my visit to her home was not anticipated by whomever was after my family and I."

"Instead of developing this elaborate plan of yours, why didn't you just call the cops?"

"With all due respect, calling the cops would have risked getting us killed. Our phones were tapped. The caller had threatened to put a bullet through my son's head! My innocent, loving son. I wouldn't dare call the police so they could tell me I was SOL without a voicemail from the caller."

"How do you know your home was bugged?"

"It had to be. They knew personal things about my family—about my son. At first, the idea was only a theory, but later I knew for sure I was right."

"How?"

"I used my cell phone to book flights to New York, for my husband and me, and that kept them quiet."

"Explain why you did that."

"To throw them off."

"Them who?"

"Our stalkers. The ones that have been threatening us. I wondered why they would call us to threaten our lives, instead of just killing us already; you know? I got the feeling that they were waiting for something—"

"Waiting for what?"

"For my mother."

"Sonia?"

"Yes. They wanted us together; I guess they planned on making us suffer. But when my mother suddenly moved to Maryland, it somehow messed up their plans. They didn't know where my mom was, and if she was coming back at all. They were waiting for me to lead them to her."

"Mrs.- I mean Lexi, could you please reaffirm where you were that night? Who saw you?"

"When I returned home, I tried to explain to my husband that I allowed Lavern to take our son to Maryland, to hide out at my mom's."

"You tried to explain to your husband?"

"Yes, he wouldn't allow me to explain why I did it. He wouldn't even allow me to explain my plan to him. He was just so mad that I hadn't returned home with our son."

"So you and your husband had a fight that evening."

"No—"

"No?"

"I mean- I wouldn't call it a fight. We had a disagreement. He told me to take the trip to New York without him."

"So he ended your relationship."

"You are fishing around for a motive, just so you can pin this shit on me, you bastard. Listen, you pig! I didn't try to kill my husband. You found a man shot to death in my backyard. You should be out there trying to catch the killer. You need to figure out what the hell he was doing in my yard to begin with, and who the hell shot him, and why! What was the motive for that? Huh? Find that out and let me know."

"Mrs. Henry, I would recommend that you cooperate with me."

"Call me Lexi! And yes! My husband and I had a fight, as all married couples do. I called a cab immediately afterward, and went to the airport."

"What is the name of the cab service you used that night?"

"New Horizon's."

"Hmm. What time did you call the cab?"

"After I went upstairs and showered. About 7:40 pm."

"At what time did the cab arrive at your home?"

"Around 7:55 pm."

"At what time did you arrive at the airport?"

"At 9:52 pm."

"Really? Interesting," Officer Lloyd checked his notes, apparently puzzled.

My heart skipped several beats. I wondered where he was going with this.

"This was the Fort Lauderdale Airport?"

"No. Miami."

"So it took you almost two hours to get to the Miami Airport from Weston?"

My heart skipped several beats.

"Maybe it's because we stopped for a while."

"Oh? May I ask why?"

"So that I could cry- get myself together."

"You ended up cancelling your flight to New York, is that accurate?"

"Yes. My intention was never to go to New York. I intended to meet Lavern and my son in Maryland."

"Ok. That will be all for today. We contacted New Horizon's and managed to get a hold of Carlos Lopez, the cabby who chauffeured you that night. He'll be coming in later this afternoon for questioning. Hopefully his story will sync up with yours. You'll be hearing from me again soon," Officer Lloyd smiled smugly.

I could hear myself swallow. I was inwardly sweating bullets. That was the last thing I'd expected to hear. I was certainly fucked. Carlos Lopez. He'd given me his phone number that night, after I warned him. *"Listen to me creep, as far as you're concerned, I never turned back. Do you hear me? I had you pull over so I could cry, but I never turned back."*

"Anything por you, my amor bonita!" he'd replied smiling and winking at me.

That's when it had hit me. The reason why he'd been staring at me so piercingly that night was because he found me attractive. I most times forgot about my good looks. When men stared at me, it usually didn't occur to me that it's because they're completely smitten. All the while I thought Carlos Lopez was up to no good.

"Mrs. Henry, are you okay?" Officer Lloyd interrupted me from my thoughts. His smug smile remained.

"I'm absolutely fantastic," I smiled smugly back at the police officer. I watched as his smile dissipated. He appeared to be stunned by my reaction.

Someone once told me, that when you're beautiful, you can get whatever you want. Carlos Lopez, I'm counting on you, my amor. He was my alibi. Should Lopez renege, I would be charged with attempted murder, and murder in the first, or second, or whatever degree. A motive has already been established for my wanting to murder my husband. It would be deemed a crime of passion.

But it was also highly likely for me to be in the clear. Lavern would testify that she witnessed me being threatened. Mom and Tyrese were also witnesses. My son had also explained to the authorities about the men in the black car who threatened him. The phone records, and murder of my grandparents; Uncle Desmond's testimony, was enough to create doubts in any juror's mind.

I had also been made aware that Uncle Desmond had been transported safely back to the United States, and was currently under medical supervision at the Broward General Hospital.

Politician Styles had been arrested for the carnage committed in the woodlands of Manchester, even though he wasn't talking. The man whom I shot to death was identified as Martin Baker, aka Kappa. The cell phone found on Kappa had linked back to an ex-con known to many as Chin. Chin's body was found along Brooklyn Shoreline in New York. Also, a briefcase that was recovered from my backyard, contained incriminating evidence against a successful attorney known as Sharp. The information was linked back to Vaughnn, Chin and Prime Minister Styles. The authorities have still not disclosed additional details about the contents of the briefcase—or anything else.

And in other news, Everhard was released from jail and was temporarily sequestered for his own safety. His testimony was invaluable.

This is why I found it amazing that the popos kept grilling me the way they did. A phone call to Lopez now would only heighten suspicions against me.

So here I was, home, watching my son sleep, and wishing JT had been killed.

CHAPTER THIRTY EIGHT
D-MONEY

I was locked up for one week. At first, I explained to the cops that I knew the law, and it was wrong of them to arrest me without a cause. But later that night they'd found the chloroform and gun at the scene of the crime where I was standing.

They now had reasons to believe that the weapons belonged to me. I had one strategy that had always worked for me. Deny, deny, deny.

There were no fingerprints found on the weapons, as I had cleaned my gun and worn my black, leather gloves prior to having them on me that night. This had been the first I'd ever seen investigators so baffled. I wasn't sure what was going on, but it seemed huge—bigger than me.

I was baffled too. I could hardly believe that Mama Dukes hadn't come to the station to rescue me. She also had not accepted any of my calls. When I returned home, she never spoke to me. Crazybitch.

This morning, a week and a half later, Officer Barkly and Officer Price showed up at my door. They asked me to accompany them to the station, so here I was.

"Damon Jenkins!" Officer Barkly shouted.

I looked up at him from my chair, wondering what the hell was about to happen next.

"I have your statement here, but there's something that doesn't sit well with me," he placed two files on the table.

"Why was your New Horizon's cab parked so meticulously in the bushes of the backstreets on the night of October 16?"

"I told you man, I saw the fire and commotion at that house and wanted to know what was going on."

"Bullshit!"

"Then you tell me what happened, Mr. All Knowing! Matter-of-fact, I won't say another word until I speak with my lawyer."

"Son of a bitch!" Officer Barkly angrily slapped the desk with his palm.

"Alright, you little fucker! You're free to go for now. But this is not over."

I strutted towards the exit with a smug smile on my face. I was pleased. The fact of the matter is, the cops had nothing on me, as much as they wished they did. I wanted Lexi and her peeps to suffer, and she already was. And I didn't even have to do a thing. I floated towards the exit victoriously. Karma was indeed a bitch. I knew that now. I smiled some more.

"Jenkins!"

I turned around and saw Officer Barkly approaching.

"You're gonna fuck up!" he smiled cynically. "And when you do, I'm going to have your ass!"

I stood there shocked that he could say shit like that, and get away with it.

"Is that all?" I asked.

"Get out of my station!" he barked.

I smiled at him. He couldn't touch me. I turned back around and resumed my stroll towards the exit.

I even smiled some more as I sauntered pass a young lady who had begun to cuss out a female officer.

"Do you fucking cops even know what you're doing?" she screamed. "How difficult could it be to find my assailants?"

"Miss Stimpson, calm down or we're gonna have to detain you," the female officer warned.

"All you had to do was locate the vehicle and find the Purple Cadillac with 22 dubs, and you would have found the four men who beat me up eight years ago, flung me in the trunk of their purple Cadillac, and then gang raped me!"

I held my breath and quickened my stride. What the hell was happening? I ran my hand through my unruly locks and panted anxiously as I neared the exit. So near, yet so far away. I was all but running towards that exit by now.

"Shut the fuck up, this can't be real!" she shouted.

"That's it Miss Stimpson, I have to arrest you—"

"No- I mean- that's him! That's one of the men who raped me! There he is! There he is!" she cried.

My heart pounded. Exit.

"Barkly, I need your help over here now!" I heard the female officer say—right before I dashed through the doors. I suddenly wished New Horizons hadn't fired me. I could use a ride right about now.

I hurried through the gates and dialed Shug-B's phone. It went straight to voicemail. Dang! Shug-B was rejecting me now, dawg?

"Jenkins! Stop where you are, and put your hands in the air!"

CHAPTER THIRTY NINE
LEXI

I stepped onto the balcony of my hotel room, inhaled deeply and allowed the cool wind to soothe my broken spirit. I exhaled and admired the majestic trees and acres upon acres of lush vegetation, and golf course.

I was staying at the Luxury Coast Hotel which was located twenty six miles away from Kingston, and approximately thirty two miles away from Mandeville. Lexington and I had arrived in Jamaica one week ago. The countdown to the event the day before had to have been one of my worst experiences ever, and as you all know, I've had tons of bad experiences. My grandparents' funeral is the event to which I'm referring. It devastated me. When I saw their golden faces in those caskets, I just lost it. What animal would so viciously kill the elderly?

Today, I was all cried out, and a hundred times more depressed. Would my heart ever heal from all the damage done? Would I ever overcome the pain?

Would the sins of my past continue to haunt me? Could I ever forgive myself for my grandparents' death?

For the first time in my life, I didn't consider my child. He was the most precious thing to have ever happened to me—certainly a blessing in my life. He'd always been a blessing, but now—I wasn't so sure. Not that I regret having Lexington, I just regret having him when I did. I wish I didn't have to face all of this—this destruction with an innocent child looking up to me. I don't think I was ready to be anybody's mama.

I wiped a stray tear from the corner of my eye and seated myself. It was good to finally be alone with my thoughts. I was grateful that mom had taken Lexington on an outing today. She'd taken him to tour the country sides, and get further acquainted with other family members. Her support since the phone threats had been phenomenal. She'd been my rock since the news of my grandparents' death. She had immediately begun working on funeral arrangements. Her husband, Tyrese, had been a huge help also, even though he didn't know my family very well.

The funeral turned out to be a huge success, thanks to mom. She'd even arranged Margaret's funeral, which was the day after my gramps'. I didn't attend Margaret's funeral. Fuck Margaret.

I was shocked to see how life had turned around, throwing ironies from left to right. For instance, my mother, who had once kicked me out of her home, believing her man over me, actually ended up living with me and my husband for a while. She was now married to a real man who supported her endeavors; a real man with whom I got along well. Tyrese had stepped in and picked up my father's slack.

Speaking of father, where the hell was my father? Where had he been all these years? I remember reaching out to him a few times, but my efforts were futile. Daddy hadn't even shown up at his own parents' funeral. Even Uncle Desmond was now a better man than he—and Uncle Desmond is a son-of-a-bitch.

How come he was still alive, instead of my gramps?

In a few days I'd return home to the States. Home to the States. Funny how I now considered America my home. It was. There was nothing left for me in Jamaica. I didn't even think there was anything left for me in America. I needed to make a move. I needed to start a new life. But where would I go? Would my past follow me there?

What about JT? What about Lexington? Will he grow up a happy kid? Will he turn out like his mother? Another irony. I always vowed to never make the same mistakes my parents did. Yet, here I was, considering the possibility of leaving my son behind—with my mother. Irony, indeed.

I was depressed. I was on the verge of a nervous breakdown. I couldn't be held responsible for my thoughts then. It just wouldn't be fair.

The funeral was guarded by the Jamaica Constabulary Force, due to the factors surrounding their deaths.

The church was jam-packed. Grandma and grandpa were obviously loved. Would anyone show up to my funeral when I die?

Speaking of showing up, why did Everhard show up at the funeral yesterday? Who gave him permission to attend? Why did he think he would get away with crossing my path?

Yesterday when I saw him, I was dumbfounded. As if my trials weren't enough. The scoundrel even had the nerve to stare me down—in a most threatening manner too. How had he gotten past the police?

Clearly too much time had passed for him to recover from the lesson I'd once taught him. The time had come again for me to teach Everhard, my ex-stepfather, another lesson. I had three more days in which to plan and execute.

Suddenly I no longer felt so depressed.

CHAPTER FORTY
EVERHARD

I and I was released from jail, praises be to the most high, Haile Selassie the first. Let god arise and let his enemies be scattered. As smoke is driven away, so driveth them away. Jah! Rastafari! Let the wicked perish at the presence of god and let the righteous exceedingly rejoice! Jah! Our father strength and redeemer who reigns ova all livin' things. Jah Rastafari!

I and I opened up the door that led to I I-getable garden. Selassie kept the herbs and I-getables while I and I was locked up by Babylon. They tried to take I freedom, but I and I was like a lamb. Rastafari looked after his own and always look out for I mon. Jah-jah have my back, yuh seet!

I flashed I locks in the cool November breeze, and allowed the warm Jamaica sun to sooth I. All I needed was some of I mon home-grown herbs. Yes, jah! Herb, weed, ganja, senseh, spliff, bighead, Marijuana—whateva you call it—I grew it in my backyard, and I planned on firin' some up in my chalice right about now! Fire!

As soon as I mon was about to relax and hold a steady meditation, I heard a loud banging. The sound was coming from around the front yard. I paused and listened. The sound got even louder.

"Everhard!" someone shouted my name.

"Bloodclaut-bombo-rassclaut, mon. What kinda living natty-dread have to be facing? Every time I mon get ready to unwind with my garden, Babylon show up at I mon door.

"Everhard!"

I decided against answering the damn door. Afterall, I deserved to have some peace.

I seated myself underneath the Guangu tree and thought back to two days ago when I saw Lexi at that funeral.

Honestly, I did not show up at that funeral just to pay respects. I didn't give two cents about Lexi or her parents, or anything to do with the likes of her. I showed up because I knew for sure that she would be at the funeral. I wanted to look the bitch in the eyes, and I did. The only drawback was that I couldn't get to deal with her the way I've always dreamed. I showed up at that funeral to make Lexi suffer, but she was surrounded. Therefore, I resolved to intimidate her with that intimidating stare of mine. When our eyes locked, all I could see was the soul of an evil bitch.

At least I managed to send her a message, which is: "I'm gonna get you one day before I die, bitch."

I jumped to my feet suddenly, at the sound of footsteps around the corner. Babylon was determined to get to me after all. The sounds of leaves breaking grew louder. I watched and waited. If it was the police, then I mon would go right back to jail when they discovered the weed I was growing in I garden.

Babylon always finds a way to punish rastaman.

"See him deh! Grab him!" A strapping, middle-aged man shouted to his armed companion.

Realizing they weren't the police, I dashed towards the entrance of the house.

"If yu run, I will shoot yu in yu foot!" the armed assailant dived towards me.

"Alright! I won't run!" I stopped in my tracks, raised my hands above my head, and turned around, heart racing, just in time to be greeted by a solid blow to my jaw. It brought me to my knees.

I spat blood and looked up.

The strapping trespasser smirked as he slowly approached.

"Wha mi do this time?" I asked in my deepest Jamaican Patois.

"Shut up!" The armed, skinny one put his gun away in his waist and reached for the leather strap from the big 'hol battybwoy.

The big ass battyboy sat on the wooden bench and reached for I mon. He dragged me towards him and told I mon to lay across his lap.

"No, rasta! Not again to bloodclaut. You will have to kill I today!" I was devastated. What the hell was all of this? Where was Selassie? Not a bloodclaut. This had Lexi's name written all over it.

"I said shut up!" the armed one retrieved his gun and held it to my head. "Climb up on his lap!"

"Murder!" I tried to yell, but my jaw was too swollen for the words to come out right.

The armed one shoved me, so that I fell face down onto his colleague's lap. I cried the living tears. I cried for Selassie. But they laughed at me and pulled my pants down. When they pulled my brief down, I lost it. I hollered like a little child. Oh, the horror of what they were about to do to me! Then I felt cold water being poured on my backside. I paused briefly to wonder what the fuck they were up to; then I resumed bawling. They continued to laugh.

"Sorry mi late, mon!" a third male shouted as he approached us.

A third male? Horrified at the position I was in, I began to put up a fight.

"Please, don't do it!" I pleaded and squirmed and writhed. Then CRACK!

My body froze in pain as soon as the leather strap collided with my wet behind. My eyes bulged as my injured jaws dropped.

"This one is for being insubordinate," the armed one said.

"Yu recording this?" the strappin' one asked.

"Yes, mon, of course!" replied the late one.

The moment the first slap fully registered, was the moment I heard another SWOOSH. Then CRACK! The leather strap landed against my ass, as firm as before. This time I bawled. Tears were blocking my eyes I couldn't see. I wanted to see what they were doing.

"Mercy!" I begged. "Selassie! Selassie! Woiee! Jesus!"

"That one was for Lexi!" my attacker gloated.

As soon as I processed those words, a third blow landed on my butt-cheeks. This time it stung so hard that I knew my flesh had been punctured. I had no more strength left to cry. It was obvious they planned on killing me.

"Get up!" the big one ordered.

"Do his hands now," the late one giggled sinisterly.

Though I was weak, I mustered up whatever little strength I had left, and rolled off of his lap onto the ground. I made sure I landed on my knees and palms, and not my ass. I was relieved to not have received another blow on it. It seemed my guess was right. They must have seen the blood and decided to stop. So, now I was also relieved that their intention was not to kill me, or even worse than that, gang rape me! Praises be to Jesus.

"Hold out your hand!"

I did as I was told. Another crack to the center of my palm. I flashed my whole arm in agony and pleaded with them to stop.

"That one was for Lexi!"

Rasta! Didn't he say that the last time?

"Hold out the other hand!"

I complied. The leather strap sounded against my left palm. More tears. While I cried like a baby, big fool, little fool, and the camera man laughed their asses off.

When their beating had been rendered, they walked away leaving me limp on the ground.

"Oh, you can pull up your pants now!" one of them yelled, and they all laughed.

"Selassie! Selassie! Jesus!" said yet another. More laughter.

Lexi Jones. If I knew half of what I know now, I wouldn't have come anywhere near you. Matter-of-fact, I wouldn't have even touched Sonia with a long stick. You and your mother are bitches. But one day, you will reap what you sow.

CHAPTER FORTY ONE
VAUGHNN

I killed a man in prison as advanced payment for a fellow convict, Atnulu, to aide in my vengeance against Lexi jones. Somewhere along the line I got screwed, and I'm still trying to figure out who screwed me.

Atnulu had assured me that he only worked with professionals, but it seemed that these professionals employed the services of amateurs. Therefore, Lexi escaped. How the fuck else could Lexi have escaped! I was again the spotlight of the FBI, police department, and news channels. Only the pope was left to talk shit about me.

Everything had gotten real messy real fast, and I was being questioned everyday by the authorities. Bonita's father had also made things worse by the carnage he committed in Jamaica. A conspiracy theory was now being developed, and I was in the middle of it all.

There was no way I'd ever get to Lexi now. I was sure that by now she had fled to New Zealand or some far away country and shit.

Lexi had escaped; my reprisal had not been satisfied, yet I had already made my payment for all the aforementioned, and now I was in the middle of deep shit.

I had been used, but someone would have to pay. I strongly felt as if Atnulu had crossed me, and I welcomed thoughts of wasting him.

He'd been the gang leader for some time now, but I decided that I would have to switch things up a bit, and get rid of him for good.

We were close enough for him to trust me with secrets—secrets that I was already using to turn gang members against him. We were secretly plotting his death.

Prior to today, I lived only for revenge against Lexi. Now I had absolutely nothing to live for. Atnulu needed to die even if it meant that I would lose my life. I would get my vengeance one way or another.

CHAPTER FORTY TWO
UNCLE DESMOND

I had been discharged from Broward General Hospital and sent home to recuperate. My funds had been depleted; however the Ministry of Justice of Jamaica footed a generous portion of my medical expenses and provided a home health aide to care for me for three days out of each week. This was the condition of the agreement I signed, with the MOJ. They ensured I was being nursed back to health, because I was a key witness, needed to testify in court against Prime Minister Styles, and Benji Smith.

I had no choice in the matter. Whether I wanted to or not, the US government would comply with the Jamaican Government's extradition request, and extradite me to Jamaica to testify.

I was grateful nonetheless, to have been so lucky. Mama and papa always told me that I was blessed. I never really considered my life that way. Being blessed took on a spiritual meaning—Christian. I never really considered Christianity, or God. I ruled my own world.

But now, I danced to the beat of a different drum. My survival was nothing short of a miracle, and miracles came from God. So I now considered God. How can I not?

Mama and papa were right, but they were now gone. They'd died a vicious death. I hadn't been much of a son to them. My wife Margaret had died as well. I hadn't been much of a husband to her. Lexi, my niece wouldn't find it in her heart to let me in; I hadn't been much of an uncle to her. I now realized that all my life I hadn't been much of anything. I hadn't been much of a man, and it was far too late to make things right.

I wouldn't even be able to make it to my parents' nor my wife's funeral. I've raised heaven and earth in an attempt to locate my brother, Byron, Lexi's father. But he's completely fallen below everyone's radar. Byron was nowhere to be found. I even checked public records online to see if he'd been locked up. Nothing.

He might have relocated to Switzerland. He used to dream of moving to Switzerland.

However, based on the looks of things with my family these days, Byron might also be dead. I wouldn't rule anything out.

So, let's see. I had lost my parents, brother, wife, niece—I almost lost my life. I'd lost love. This was no way for anyone to live. I might as well have died in those woodlands with mama and papa.

I wanted my parents back. I desperately needed to make things right with Lexi—get her to amend her judgment of me. But how will I ever succeed—when vengeance has always been her only verdict?

CHAPTER FORTY THREE
LEXI

I realize that the good people always die and leave the evil ones to live so they can eventually suffer. My grandparents were given a worthy funeral. I was pleased with that. They had only met my son, Lexington once, but at least they had met him. They died knowing their grandson. I was hurt by the loss, even more hurt that Uncle Desmond's life had been spared. But the wicked shall suffer. There was no forgiving Desmond. He was the cause of all of this. I would never forgive him.

Mother often warned that I should release myself from the hatred I harbored for Desmond. She advised I'd be happier and free, and blah, blah. But I just couldn't do it. That would require strength, and I had no more strength left- especially now that my grandparents were gone. No. There was no forgiving Desmond. Furthermore, where was my father throughout all of this? He hadn't even shown up to his parents' funeral, in Jamaica. Was he dead too? I'd gotten so used to not having a father, that I'd forgotten he existed.

Parents should man up and support their children through college before throwing them out into the world after high school. The law states that, at eighteen years old, a person is an adult, ready for the world. But that law is bullshit. What does one know at eighteen that he or she didn't know at seventeen? High school does not prepare a child for the world. College does. I know that my duties as a parent will not have expired once my child graduates high school. I will not punk out of my responsibilities as a loving parent, just because the law says.

As we were entering JT's room, a doctor was making his exit.

"Doctor," I held Lexington's little hands and hurried towards the doctor.

"Yes?" he paused and waited.

"I- I am Mr. Henry's wife."

"Oh, Mrs. Henry. I'm Doctor Lee," he extended his hand.

"Yes doc, I- wanted to know how he's been doing," I shook his hand, wishing he'd keep his hospital germs to himself. I've always hated hospitals.

"He's been asking for you. Mr. Henry is a fighter."

"So- is he really that bad?" I felt indifferent, but I was curious nonetheless.

"His condition is critical—he received severe third degree burns, and some fourth degree."

"Doctor, what does this mean? Will he die?"

"Well- his condition does seem hopeful. He's definitely not out of the woods as of yet; however, like I said, Mr. Henry is a fighter. Skin grafting will be necessary."

"Skin graft?"

"Yes. We will utilize a donor or a skin bank to obtain a good match for your husband."

"Why will he need donated skin?"

"Due to the severity of his injuries, there wasn't enough healthy skin left on him to perform the procedure."

"Really? So- besides skin graft, is there anything else"—"

"Absolutely," Doctor Lee said, cutting me off. "So far he's in stable condition, but your husband has a long fight ahead of him. We treated the burns and applied bandages so that his wounds would not get infected. The bandages also helped to make him more comfortable. He is in extensive pain, so we have to continually medicate him. Rehabilitation will eventually be needed to restore his ability and quality of life. He has lost partial sight in his left eye, but I assure you, he's in good hands. We are doing all that we can for your husband."

"Oh."

"Mrs. Henry, are you ok?"

"I am."

"I'm surprised you haven't visited your husband since—"

"Lexington, are you ready to say hello to your daddy?" I said, cutting off Dr. Lee.

Lexington nodded his head. He had been asking to see JT for weeks now, and I have run out of excuses for why he can't.

"I think that's it for now, doc; thank you so much."

"You're welcome," the doctor replied before scurrying away puzzled.

I waited until he was out of site before entering JT's room.

I wiped tears from my eyes, knelt down to kiss my son.

The sight of JT frightened me- us. Lexington screamed and clung to my legs.

I glanced at JT who could only blink in agony. His life was over. He loved his son, but the cocky bastard was in no position to care for a child. He'd never see his son again, after today. I lifted Lex into my arms and whispered into his ears.

Moments later, he was calm. I approached JT who continued to blink.

"JT, I brought your son to see you."

"Shank- ou," he blinked.

"You're welcome," I replied. "Lex, say hello to your daddy."

"Hello, daddy," Lex said, without looking at JT.

I observed JT's reaction to this. Blink, blink, blink.

My psyche adjusted to the sight of him.

"I'm sure you're glad to be alive," I said, and watched as he continued to blink. Tears escaped his right eye.

"Ok, honey, I'm taking you outside to sit with grandma, ok?" I carried Lex to Grandma, who were seated in the wait area.

I returned to JT.

He was wrapped from head to toe, like an Egyptian mummy. Only his eyes, ears, nose and mouth were visible. The doctors said he was partially blind in his left eye. He required several major surgeries, and would require intensive therapy to learn how to function normally again.

It had been six weeks, since the murder attempt against his life. I'd finally mustered up the courage to see him, for the first and last time. I was moving to Antigua, and I planned on taking my son with me.

"Wot too-ou so long?"

"What took me so long to come see you?"

He blinked.

"Well- you broke up with me, so I didn't think you really wanted to see me."

"Yex-shee-"

"Yes?"

"ou maiee ife."

"I was your wife. But you broke up with me. Remember what you told Carlecia? Oh, yeah- that you couldn't stand the thought of spending your life with a bitch like me. Do you remember?"

He blinked away tears.

"I'm moving away to Antigua. I'm taking my son- and don't look at me like that. Once you are well again, you can come get him. I'm leaving all my information with mom."

"Yex-shee, ee are est fiends."

My name is Lexi, dammit. LEXI! We were best friends, but not anymore. I know what you did- have us kicked out of the Witness Protection Program just so you could screw Carlecia."

I watched as he blinked through more tears. I felt sorry for my son's father. But that sympathy was lessened by the facts I knew about him. He was a scoundrel, fact. He was ungrateful, fact. He caused my grandparents to die, fact. I was manless because of him, fact. He used me in every way and then tried to dispose of me like trash, fact. He was a cocky bastard, fact. The list about him goes on and on, fact.

"Is there anyone that you would like me to call? Maybe- one or two of your girlfriends?"

"Yex-shee," he repeated.

"It's Lexi. Say Lexi," I replied icily.

"I know ou dee deesh oo nee."

"Excuse me? You know I did what to you?"

"I guesh I deser deesh."

I remained silent. I didn't know if anyone deserved that, especially JT. But why the hell should I care now, when JT played me all these years?

"I fo-give ou. 'lease take cay of ow song."

I bent over and lightly kissed the bandages on his forehead. Then proceeded to make my exit. As I was heading out, Wendy appeared out of nowhere. She stopped to look at me.

Without skipping a beat, I doubled back and swung my arm forward; delivering a punch to her face that sent her sprawling on the floor. I flew out of there and sailed past my mother and son in the waiting room.

"Mom! Tyrese! Grab Lexington and let's go!" I yelled as I sprinted through the lobby, leaving everyone looking confounded.

Who is Lexi? Who am I?

I was sailing north on Interstate-95.

I eyed my rearview mirror and observed Tyrese's car about a mile behind.

Back at the Bella Villa Inn, Carlos Lopez was waiting for me. He'd come through for me after all, and had certified my alibi. We'd become close friends. He planned on moving to Antigua with me and my son.

Tyrese would be flying mom over to see me often.

Lavern relocated to Coconut Creek, Florida. Surprisingly she wished to rekindle our friendship, but I had no use for those who had no use for my son.

This time tomorrow, Lopez, Lexington and I would be on a plane to beautiful Antigua.

Tomorrow was the beginning of a new life. Hopefully we would get the fresh start we anticipated, and build new memories.

Speaking of memories, I pulled over onto an off ramp to quickly check my cell phone. For the millionth time I watched the video of Everhard getting his butt whipped. I anticipated the smile the recording would put on my face. I fast forwarded to my favorite part.

"Selassie! Selassie! Woiee! Jesus!"

Just as expected, a small smile parted my lips— for the one millionth time.

EPILOGUE
JT

Two years have passed since my tragedy. My healing is and will always be ongoing. I've undergone a series of surgeries and currently have a million more to look forward to.

When I look at myself in the mirror to date, I see a monster. I know it's ludicrous to have fought the good fight for my son's sake, yet, at the end of it all, I'm too scared to let him see me this way.

All of my functionalities have been weakened. My life no longer held meaning to me; I was no longer surviving for my son. Lexington was gone from me forever.

The woman closest to me had devastated my life. All the women I once knew had disappeared. I even took a chance and sent Tanisha a recent picture of me. The divorce between Lexi and I was finalized thirteen months ago, so I looked forward to marrying Tanisha. I believed in Tanisha and her ability to accept me for who I am.

But I believed wrong. Tanisha has changed her phone number, and can no longer be reached. Ain't that some shit!

All I was now left with is my restaurant. I'm grateful because it keeps me afloat—puts food on my table, and allows me to remain in hiding. I want to crawl into a hole and disappear.

My son occupies my thoughts. He's now seven years old, and has probably forgotten about his daddy. It's probably for the best because I have given up on him. I don't think I will be fighting my ex-wife for my son. Why would any child choose a monster over his mother?

I think about my daddy. I often wonder if he's turning in his grave.

How I was still alive—and kept going from day to day, and why, remained a mystery to me.

No number of surgeries or amount of healing will ever restore me to my old self. This is who I was now, and I needed to deal with it.

It's ironic to see how I'd refused to be with certain women due to my fear of their volatility; while all the time I'd been living with the most unpredictable bitch of all. I've always known that she had set the fire. She had gotten away with it, and the blame placed on Vaughnn, Prime Minister Styles, and their accomplices. Lexi had somehow conjured a solid alibi. A cab driver. Really?

I could easily hunt down Lexi, and get vengeance. But I wouldn't. This is where it all ends.

There was also no saving my son. It was too late. He was already under his mother's influence.

How can my son not be doomed when his mother has taught him that vengeance is the only verdict?

The End

Thanks for being a fan!

Please spread the good word about Tanisha J. Beecher Bell in any way you can.

Please visit https://www.rsvipllc.com/book-store to learn more about my current and upcoming work-- and me.

www.ingramcontent.com/pod-product-compliance
Lightning Source LLC
Chambersburg PA
CBHW021137110726

47900CB00002B/387